A Fairy-Tale Christmas

By:
Stephanie Guerrero

ISBN-13: 9781691676446

"For you were once darkness,
but now **you are light in the Lord. Live as children of light**

(for the fruit of the light consists in all goodness, righteousness and truth) and find out what pleases the Lord." ~Ephesians 5:8-10

Chapter One

Marionette Goldberg placed her hands on her hips and fought back against the heavy burden of leadership. She could not carry on like this forever. Frustration loomed like a dark cloud waiting to take hold at the first hint of despair. Glancing across the office pool, to the other side of the massive room of cubicles, her eyes fell on an attractive thirty something man with his head in his hands.

A problem means a solution. She'd prayed. She knew what needed to be done, but the ability to convince others eluded her. Mitch Ajax Torres possessed all the qualities she sought, the problem… the board saw his PTSD from time embedded with the troops as an eliminator. So far, nothing persuaded them. The situation called for creativity.

Tapping a slender finger against her chin, she pondered the problem. Since her father's death, control of his media conglomerate fell to her as well as left a giant whole in the Editor-in-Chief role. Keeping his finger on the pulse of the world as Editor-in-Chief of the global paper typified her father's passion, but doing everything exhausted her.

Just because I can do something, doesn't mean I should. Wisdom dictated she find a great editor.

Inspiration struck. With December approaching, instigating a mandatory Secret Santa drawing for the news staff promised to build moral and force Torres to interact with his co-workers.

She went into action immediately. Before the noon hour, each staff member received a memo with a personal information form to be filled out and returned by the end of the day. By lunchtime, a merry, holiday buzz filled the office. Jokes and teasing rose from the cubicles as individuals filled out their forms. One by one, each form found its way to the desk of the administrative assistant. All but one found her desk by the end of the day… Torres. His move called for a serious countermove. She smiled at the challenge.

~

The boss' administrative assistant knocked on his open door. Mitch forced his shoulders back and prepared to dig in his heels. Participating in a jolly Christmas game…? Not happening. Compared to all the visions bouncing around in his head, a Secret Santa game felt trivial. Besides, he couldn't deal with people right now. Surviving daily required all his energy. He growled at the prim young woman he remembered from his college days.

"What is it? Did the boss send you to reprimand me for not jumping into the game?" he groused.

Isabella Farias pushed black-framed glasses up on her delicate nose and frowned at him. That act alone hit home. Though their paths rarely crossed, Isabella always sported a brilliant smile. In fact, he rubbed his scruffy chin; he never saw her with a frown. Knowing he put the frown there stung. He straightened and tried again.

"Sorry, Isabella. I'm a bear lately. Any chance the boss lets me off this particular assignment? I'm more grinch than Santa this year," he admitted through gritted teeth.

Her soft, understanding smile returned at his honesty.

"The boss understands your position, Mitch and knows it's been a difficult year. The whole office needs a boost in morale since the owner's untimely death last year. The memo isn't optional. In fact, I've been asked to add a second name for you to gift. One of your co-workers left town due to a family member's heart surgery which leaves things uneven."

She thrust two forms his direction. He stared. "Are you serious? I'm not in any position to take care of buying a stranger a gift, let alone two!" he stood and raised his voice. "Tell the boss 'no way'!"

"That's just the point, Mitch. You've isolated yourself. We are family here at the paper, yet you just called your co-workers strangers. The boss insisted. This is *not* optional, and you *will* take on these two ladies." She placed the papers on his desk and turned to go.

"Ladies! Are you kidding me? At least I might have a clue with a guy! I don't even know where to start!"

She pointed to his desk. "Everything you need to know is right there, Mitch. One gift a week until Christmas. I'll let the boss know you are on it." She paused in the doorway.

"I'll keep your reluctance to myself… for now. Just do right by these two names."

~

Two days later, Mitch ripped the paper off a package left by his office Secret Santa and winced.

Great… just what I always wanted… a unicorn mug, complete with horn and a rainbow tale for a handle.

Hot pink block letters wrapped around the white body of the mug with one word… FIERCE! A grunt escaped his normally stoic lips. At least his co-worker got that part right. For allowing himself to be conned into this stupid tradition, he could kick himself, but the memo from the boss stated that the veteran war correspondent needed to connect with the rest of the writing staff. He shook his head and crumbled the multicolored, glittered tissue paper, lobbing the ball into his sleek stainless steal trash can.

He picked up the unicorn mug prepared to trash it, but entertained second thoughts. Did he dare regift it? He glanced around the office pool and decided against it. No telling who gifted the mug to him. Anyone could be responsible. One of the guys could have pranked him, or one of the ladies might have attempted to make him smile. He turned the mug over in his hands and felt the corners of his lips crack at the attempt to curve. The gift *almost* worked. He made the sudden decision to flaunt the mug around the office.

Stepping out of his glassed-in office and holding his pet mug by the tail, he made his way passed the cubicles to the break room for coffee. Smiles and smirks broke as he passed. He raised the mug in a grand salute and stepped in to pour a cup of coffee. He pondered his current Secret Santa assignment. What should he get the women his list?

A copy of each of their likes rested on his desk, a form the boss forced him to fill out as well. His form, hastily inscribed, lacked the item currently resting in his hand. Unicorns never made the cut, still… a guy could do worse than having a girl's list of favorite things handed to him on silver platter. The two names he received couldn't be more different from each other or from him.

Caitlyn Roberts stepped into the breakroom, took one look at his mug and raised an eyebrow. The fiery, redheaded beauty never missed an opportunity to use her quick wit at his expense. Why she picked on him, she couldn't say. As near as he could figure, she fought hard to keep her position and kept all the guys at arm's length. With one exception… she teased him mercilessly. And of course, her name appeared on his desk.

"Lose a bet?" the local crime reporter smirked and raised her 'I don't do Mondays… or Tuesdays… etc.' mug in salute. He grinned. The mug fit her sarcasm.

"Nah, Roberts, haven't you heard? Boss says I

need to be more approachable. Is it working?" Pulling a couple of tickets from his jacket pocket, he waved them in her face. "Want to go out, Friday night? I have tickets to the hockey game of the season," he poked fun. "Oh… that's right. You don't date co-workers."

The redhead snatched the tickets from his hand and studied them in awe. "How'd you get these, Torres? The game's been sold out for months!"

Jax grinned and took a slow sip out of his unicorn before answering. "I have connections. Jealous?"

Caitlyn narrowed her brown eyes. "How about we work a deal? Is there someone you need investigated?"

Downing the rest of his coffee, Jax stepped to the sink and took his time rinsing out his new mug. He could feel Caitlyn salivating over his tickets. Truth be told, he hated going to a game alone, but since his last stint in Afghanistan, most of the guys he knew were married or were no longer in touch. He ran his eyes over the fiery redhead.

Her ever present pony-tail and worn ballcap advertising for the Yankees rubbed him wrong. A more diehard Mets fan than he would be hard to find. Jeans, Converse sneakers with a plaid shirt over a tee proclaiming her a 'daddy's girl' completed her athletic, no-nonsense appearance. Except for the hair and trim figure, she could be one of the guys.

"Aw… come on, Torres. Do a girl a favor. I'd owe you big time. My older brothers have done nothing but gripe about their lack of tickets for weeks."

Having the stubborn crime beat reporter owe him definitely influenced his decision, but he snatched his tickets back and waved them in her face just to be stubborn.

"Surely, a guy like you needs help with the whole Secret Santa gig," she pressed. "I hear your stubborn streak landed you with two names in the Secret Santa gig."

"Wait, how do you know I have more than one name in the Secret Santa game?" his voice filled with suspicion.

She refilled her mug and tapped her temple. "Trade secret. Investigative reporter… remember."

"More like snoop…" he muttered.

"so… do we have a deal? I'll buy the hot dogs…" she pressed.

"I'll think on it."

"Fair enough… you know where my desk is," she saluted and slipped passed him.

~

How should she sign her cards? 'Good fairy'… too whimsical? 'Secret Santa'… too classic? 'Wouldn't you like to know who'… too fiery? The truth? He needed to laugh, know someone cared, and to tap into a sentimental side he rarely showed. She knew his romantic side existed. Starting with making him laugh turned out to be a great choice. His response surprised her in the best way. He accepted the unicorn mug with charm.

Her goal for the month: draw him out of hiding.

Since coming back from his last assignment, Mitch avoided gatherings. She missed his former optimism around the office. Fairy tale reminders permeated the thought behind every gift. He required a reminder that dreams can come true.

A deep croak emitted from the aerated container setting beside her on the passenger seat of her Jeep. A chuckle escaped her lips. Lately, Mitch exhibited traits of a frog rather than a prince. Pulling into the staff parking lot, she slipped into the building and jogged the four floors to enter the writers' pool unseen. With a clandestine glance around the quiet room, she dodged and dashed through the cubicles before reaching the war correspondent's office. She hurriedly left her package and dashed back to her desk passing Mitch just as he exited the breakroom. As usual, the man didn't even acknowledge her existence unless forced to for business. She shrugged. All the better for playing his Secret Santa.

Caitlyn Roberts paused by her desk. The fiery redhead intimidated some, but in reality… the woman would die for her closest friends.

"Hey, Izzie…" Bella winced at the pet name. "Want to go to lunch? Italian or Greek food? There's this little joint a couple blocks away. The souvlaki is amazing!"

Hoping to get some form of reaction out of her gift recipient, Bella gave a distracted nod. "Yeah… sure, Caitlyn." Forcing herself to pay attention, she turned her eyes to meet Caitlyn's raised eyebrow.

"How about I meet you there at 11:30? I have a few things left to do to meet my deadline."

The beat reporter crossed her arms. "Uh huh…

who is he, Izzie?"

She shook her head in denial. "Lay off. It's not like that, Caitlyn. Look, I'll meet you at 11:30, okay?"

Caitlyn threw up her hands. "Okay! Just let me know if you need me to pound anyone for you. I've got your back. Remember what I did to the last guy who broke your heart?"

Bella sighed. "Yeah... exposed his gambling tendencies, his faint connections to the mob, got him fired and five years in the state pen. Really, Caitlyn, he broke my heart when I found out about his favors for the mob, but I'm the one who broke up with him, remember?"

Shrugging, Caitlyn backed away with a grin. "He broke your heart, Izzie. That's crime enough in my book. The fact that he committed crimes, made putting him away easy and his own fault. Besides... it's what I do! See you at 11:30." With a salute, she strolled away just as a roar rumbled from Jax's office.

Ducking her head back into her computer, she grinned. Lately, Mitch buried his emotions. If she got him to smile, yell, or any form of emotion, she succeeded in part. "Aww... wee lamb..." she chuckled as the grumblings got louder.

Chapter Two

Emerging from a rough night and a rougher morning, Mitch rubbed the five o'clock shadow he neglected to shave, stared at the large, green gift bag sitting on his desk and opened the card. Unicorn glitter sprinkled across his office chair. He growled.

What is it with this Secret Santa and unicorns? He muttered. Opening the card, his eyes settled on the handwriting. He noticed a difference from last week. Last time letters cut from a magazine formed the note. This time, block lettering filled the page.

WE ALL HAVE A CHOICE TO MAKE
WHEN WE'RE BLUE
ACT A PRINCE AMONG MEN
OR CROAK AND YELL, ITS TRUE!
WHICH ONE ARE YOU?

He peeked over the decorative bag just as a loud croak echoed from the bag. He cried out and jumped back. His nerves were still on high alert since the battlefield. Irritation rose, along with his blood pressure. What kind of Secret Santa would pull such a prank? More prepared, he tried again.

Sure enough, a giant bullfrog sat in an aerated container. A sleek cherry wood box sat beside the frog with a note attached.

"For such a prince among men… its been awhile. I'd love to see this on you."

It couldn't be… A Blake's silk tie? The emblem stamped on the wood verified his once held dream to own a Blake's tie. *But I don't even remember mentioning this desire in the last couple of years.*

Holding his breath, he ignored the frog and carefully lifted the box out of the bag, simultaneously prying the lid open. Delight found root in the dry ground of his heart. Emerald-green silk, embossed with royal purple and gold designs shimmered even under the terrible office lighting. He couldn't remember the last time he wore a tie, but this one… he used to dream of owning a tie like this. He sank into his ergonomic office chair. Where had that man gone?

Shaking his head, he pulled the frog container out and set it on his desk before checking the bag one more time. He grinned. Of course, the bottom of the gift bag sported candy kisses. For a frog to turn prince, a kiss *must* be involved. His Secret Santa hoped for a transformation. Popping a dark chocolate into his mouth, he sighed.

Though he originally wanted to punch his gifter at finding a live bull frog in his gift, the dream tie and the kisses worked their magic. He slipped out of his office with the croaking frog amidst incredulous stares and a few grins and jogged down the stairs and out the door to the small pond across the street.

A concrete bench at the water's edge provided

the perfect spot to sit. Popping open the frog's container, he urged the creature out into the open finally dumping the animal back into the pond. The crisp December air hinted at snow. He sucked in a breath and stared at the water. Taking time to pause and stare at nature for a moment felt good.

Shaking off the knots in his shoulders, he stood and forced his steps back inside and into the restroom. The mirror's reflection stung. Staring at his unshaven, long-haired mess of a face, he made a decision. Buttoning his open collar, he used the mirror, and tied a Windsor knot.

He gave the gift giver credit. So far, a smile cracked his lips at the unicorn mug, and a tie graced his neck for the first time in years, not to mention the small breath of nature and fresh air. He sucked in another breath and glanced in the mirror before stepping out in front of his colleagues. *I could start a trend*, he thought chuckling. He shook his head. He needed to do a better job as a secret Santa.

Maybe I should take Roberts up on her offer to help, he mused. Leaving the bathroom, he stepped out into the maze of cubicles in search of the beat reporter's desk. He found her leaning against the desk of a fellow international correspondent chatting up a breeze. Some luck. Roberts's upbeat, no-nonsense attitude and flaming hair stood in stark contrast to the olive-skinned, blue-eyed, raven haired co-worker. Though rarely catching Adeline in the office, Mitch remembered her from his rookie days, from her byline and now her Secret Santa bio.

He scanned Addie's cubicle looking for extra clues to the correspondent's likes and dislikes. From her form, Adeline preferred Turkish coffee or Mexican cocoa as her drinks of choice, appreciated fine art, floral sundresses, and French pastries. Her articles were always factually accurate, politically inciteful and personally moving. A bouquet of sunflowers in a mason jar surprised him. The collection of first edition Edgar Rice Burroughs novels did not. Everything about the woman breathed first class. He definitely needed help here.

Roberts glanced up first and smirked.

"Ready to share those tickets, Jax?"

Frustrating woman. Adeline suddenly met his eyes. Her blue eyes dropped to his tie and back up to greet him with a soft smile that lit up the small space.

"The tie looks good on you, Mitch. How long since you've worn one?" She shook her head. "We are both out of the office so much. Forgive me if I'm mistaken." She looked between the two of them. "What tickets? And who is Jax, Caitlyn?" she looked around confused.

The redhead rolled her brown eyes. "The full name of this gentleman standing here is Mitchell Ajax. I call him Jax because it gets under his skin," she chuckled. "He has tickets I want to a certain game. I'm hoping to bribe him into sharing by giving him pointers on the Secret Santa names he drew. That is why you popped in, right, Jax?" She raised an eyebrow.

Leaning on Adeline's cubicle, her stance exuded confidence and grated on Mitch's nerves. Roberts could be a pal until she fixated on something, and right now her eagle instincts were locked on his tickets. Time for a tactic change. He turned toward his counter-part, "Actually, I thought I'd ask Adeline to lunch. We've been on opposite ends of the globe, and the boss is wanting me to reconnect."

Dark corkscrew curls bounced as Adeline sucked in a surprised breath. "You stopped by to ask *me* to lunch, Mitch?" Her eyes sought Caitlyn's. The redhead nodded with a wink in his direction.

"We can team up another day, Addie. Go have fun. You've earned it."

Giving Mitch a two fingered salute and a nod, Roberts stepped away.

Addie shot him a quick look and a grin. "You successfully got rid of the evil queen, Mitch. You don't have to take me to lunch. You're off the hook." She turned back to her typing.

Guilt trickled down the back of his spine. Placing his hand over hers, he snagged her attention. "Guilty, but look… I'm sorry, Addie. I have every intention of taking you to lunch. What's your favorite? We haven't caught up in years, and in spite of my making a sorry mess of things, the boss really is on my back to reconnect with my office-mates."

~

He chose to wear the tie. She smiled and listened to the man's awkward attempt to outmaneuver a maneuver. He paled and tugged at the new tie as Adelaide released him from lunch. Though awkward, Mitch remained a gentleman. The thought soothed her heart as she watched the two head out the door to lunch.

A slight sigh escaped her lips. She wanted to see him smile for real. Would it be terrible if he directed that smile at her? She noticed Mitch in grad school… something about which he seemed clueless. Though in a campus Bible study group of around fifty people, their paths crossed only a hand full of times back then. Their few interactions involved his teasing her in some manner. She missed it.

She straightened the papers on her desk and opened the mail. Mitch, or Jax, she chuckled, fearlessly jumped into life with both feet; or he used to before embedding with the troops overseas. She missed his pranks, missed his hopeful spirit. The cautious, somber man who returned was *not* an improvement. She bit her lip.

Okay, maybe his new thoughtful, measured side added stability to his happy-go-lucky nature; but she missed his carefree love of life. Mitch lived as a man of God, a prince among men, yet each day his joy vanished a little bit more. Forcing him into the Secret Santa mixer proved a God-ordained moment, almost like a calling. Laughter, inspiration, courage, joy, hope… those were the gifts she placed on his desk.

She pondered the next one and slipped out of the office, using her lunch break to donate to a local soup kitchen in his name… one she knew from years past he often served. Rushing back up the office stairs, she pondered the fact they'd asked after him. It told a story. Mitch was retreating. She tucked a typed note inside the envelope and tied a ribbon around it for festive purposes. This gift, though not funny, reminded that courage meant something, and each small act of giving mattered. She smiled.

The actual mixer asked for one gift a week during the month of December, but she couldn't help it! She loved to give, and each gift to Mitch brought joy to her own heart. Two in one week…? Okay, so two gifts might be too much, but why not? Slipping into the mail room, she left the envelop on the mail cart to be delivered rather than take a chance at getting caught. Taking a moment to pray, she sucked in a deep breath. Shoulders back, she made her way through the office maze just in time to see Mitch and Adelaide return with takeout and part ways with a wave. He turned without a second glance and strode in her direction across the office.

Bella ducked into the breakroom and poured a cup of coffee she didn't need hoping to avoid the man. And… of course… Mitch followed her in and, grabbing his unicorn mug, stepped up to the coffee pot.

"Afternoon…" he rubbed the darkening five o'clock shadow and pushed back hair grown longer than his usual high and tight cut. He nodded her direction, and she felt her knees grown weak as he poured the dark liquid into his mug and added a bit of cream.

"You were out of town. Last week." His gruff voice and the fact he noticed caught her off guard. He jerked his head toward the reporter cubicles. "I think the entire office missed you."

She felt her jaw drop in surprise. "Really?" she

whispered mesmerized by the stirring motion of his small spoon. Her eyes jerked to his. He gave a slight answering smile. A slight one… but there, nonetheless. The coffee in her mug began to shake as she engaged the man of her dreams in conversation. Hope kindled.

Mitch met her eyes with concern. "Hey, are you okay?" He steadied her hand and removed the coffee mug. "I haven't seen you this nervous since finals week, Izzie."

Knock her over with a feather, he remembered? He raised one handsome dark brown eyebrow and the corner of his full lips lifted in a dry smile as he set her mug down on the counter beside them. "What…? Did you think I'd forgotten you, mi Bella?" The teasing nickname she once cherished from their days in the large, college Christian club rolled off his lips for the first time. She couldn't speak.

"Surprised? I've been in a funk since I got back from overseas. For some reason, seeing you today reminded me of better days." He rubbed his chin in thought. "I've been getting these crazy gifts lately, crazy, yet thoughtful. You know… I thought I'd hate this Secret Santa game, but in reality, I've been blessed." He looked her over again.

"Sorry if I scared you, Bella. I wondered… I'm not good at gift giving, but the person who drew my name is really doing a great job. Giving a gift card or chocolate to someone just doesn't seem enough after receiving such thoughtful gifts."

She finally found her tongue and smiled. "Honestly, I thought you'd forgotten or at least misplaced the memories of our time in school. I know we were never close, but I've missed your teasing, Mitch," she grinned. "Or should I call you, Jax? I hear it's trendy, you know."

Eyebrows wrinkled in a wince. "Trendy, huh." He cocked his head and scanned her up and down. "Well, I suppose turn about is fair play. I've called you Izzie plenty of times just to harass you."

She took a sip of her coffee and sputtered. She'd forgotten the cream. Turning to the fridge, she pulled out the half and half, and nodded for him to continue as she poured the cream into her mug.

"You mentioned the Secret Santa gifting being a challenge... how can I help?"

Leaning his hip against the cheap white counter, he held his hand out for the half and half carton. "I'll take some of that. Anyway, I drew two names. The Boss thought it would be a laugh to give me the spare name when one of the guys dropped out. One lady is tough enough, but two..." he rolled his eyes and poured the cream before shoving the container back into the already over-crowded employee refrigerator.

She nodded toward the breakroom table, glancing at the clock. Ten minutes left of her lunch hour. A few minutes with Mitch would be worth the lack of calories. A stale Christmas cookie constituted lunch, right?

Mitch sat down beside her and pulled the two bio sheets out of his pocket. His eyes jerked to hers suddenly. "Bella... are you part of the office game? I don't want to spoil anything."

A slow smile quirked at the corner of her lips as

she struggled to conceal her merry secret. "Like you, I volunteered at the last minute to help with overflow. One extra name needed tending, but I myself never submitted a bio, so you are safe," she whispered.

He handed her the two bios and crossed his arms as she studied them. "That hardly seems fair, Izzie. You should get Christmas gifts, not just give them." He snapped his fingers.

"I have an idea! Do you like hockey? I have tickets to the big game this week and no one to share them with."

Isabella looked up from the bio sheets in curiosity. "I thought you were taking Roberts? She's been spreading the word, and who wouldn't! This game should be the best in a while!"

Irritation spread across his tanned face. He furrowed his brow and bit his lip. "I never made her any promises or took her up on the proposed deal. I almost accepted this morning, but she acted so cocky, I never made the offer. What do you say? I'll take you to the game of the decade, feed you something better than that stale cookie you're currently munching on, and in exchange, you have mercy on me and help me with these gifts?"

"Caitlyn will be madder than a wet hen…"

He nodded. "Probably, but she shouldn't have made assumptions, and for all her faults, she doesn't hold a grudge. The tickets are mine to share, and I choose you. How about it, Izzie? Pick you up at… 6pm, Friday?"

"Mitch, I'd love to go, but you don't have to pick me up. I can meet you somewhere," she insisted, her voice just above a whisper.

He reached for the bios and paused. "Afraid I'll see where you live, Isabella?"

Her eyes widened at his words that clearly hit the mark.

"You work in an office of investigative journalists. I've noticed that you keep a low profile. It's the *why* I don't understand. You have a lovely, welcoming place. Are you still at the same flat from grad school? I seem to recall stopping off after a Bible study with a number of college students for Christmas cookie decorating or something… on the eastside?"

Could her jaw drop any lower? "You remember that?"

He shot her a quizzical look. "Of course, I do. For a guy with no family at Christmas, it's still one of my favorite memories. For one moment, family surrounded me." He pulled her to her feet and checked his watch. "Friday, I get to return the favor. Gotta run."

"Wait, Mitch…" He halted dead in his tracks.

"I have an idea for Caitlyn from her Secret Santa. The company has access to the game, and the Boss isn't using the tickets. Do you want me to see if I can secure those seats for Caitlyn from her 'Secret Santa'?"

His eyes widened and a slow grin pulled at the corner of his lips. He snatched up her hand and kissed it.

"Isabella, you are brilliant! I look forward to the game Friday, he winked. "See you at 6pm." He tapped the doorframe on his way out and strode back into the office with a confident step.

Taking a slow sip of her overly creamy coffee, Isabella plopped back down into the breakroom chair. Did Mitch Torres really just ask her to the most sought-after game of the year with the promise of dinner out. And… he not only remembered her, but carried fond memories.

Thank you, Lord, she whispered with a glance toward heaven. Draining the last of her coffee, she rinsed out the mug and headed back to her office to finish a few details. A burst of excitement shot through her. She planned to wear her team jersey for the night's festivities in anticipation of watching the game. Now, she could surprise Mitch with her sporty attire.

~

Marionette answered the call of her most difficult board member.

"Yes, what may I do for you, Susan?"

The shrill voice came through loud and clear. "What are you up to, Marion? I just passed Mitchell Torres in his office. The man's hair is as neat as you please and he's wearing a tie from one of the world's most exclusive makers! It's a complete transformation. He even stuck his head out and engaged the crime reporter in a conversation. What did you do?"

"The Secret Santa game is boosting moral all over the office," she replied. "Perhaps it's the pick-me-up Mr. Torres needed as well. We all need hope on occasion."

"Well... I don't expect his mood to last, but I hope this attitude continues. Even I'll admit the man is an amazing writer. I might be tempted to give him another look if he can keep his act together."

A thrill of praise rose from Marion's heart to heaven. Mitch exuded leadership and excellence in all he did. She sent up a prayer for the restoration of hope and healing of his wounded soul.

"That's wonderful news, Susan. Keep an eye on him for me, please."

"I'm on it. You know me... I won't vote yes unless I'm sure."

"I'm counting on it, Susan. We want God's man for the job, not just anyone. Pray."

The woman mumbled a begrudging affirmation and hung up.

Change filled the air. She sent another prayer toward heaven and let the weight of her burdens roll away to the foot of the throne of God. Reaching for a paper that needed her signature, she allowed a private grin.

~

Chapter Three

Regrets swirled in Mitch's weary brain. The back and forth of endless options overwhelmed a brain looking for safety. The decision to invite Bella to the hockey game over Caitlyn tortured him. Did he make the right choice? Going with Caitlyn ranked right up with a guys' night out.

Inviting Bella… constituted a date with someone far out of his league. The interest began years ago… that night at the cookie decorating, he almost asked her out. Until he chickened out. Yep, Caitlyn would have been the safer choice. But did he really want safe? Pulling up to Bella's 5th Avenue flat intimidated his already overly stressed brain.

"This is a bad idea, Jax," he mumbled even as he snatched the keys from the ignition and bolted toward her door. Blowing out a breath, he shook off the nerves. *No guts, no glory,* he repeated and pounded on the blue door.

The door opened, and he sucked in a breath. This perfect combination of hockey fan, complete with jersey, and hot date complete with rosy lipstick and a messy ponytail blew his second thoughts out of the water. An adorable sports fan replaced the conservative, prim and proper administrative assistant.

He swallowed hard and felt a slow, ridiculous grin tug at the corners of his mouth. If this previewed the night to come, he might have just made the best decision of his life. Light fell on the tiny gold cross in the hollow of Bella's neck as a reminder that beauty is more than skin deep. He offered his arm.

"Wow! You look… ready for the game, mi Bella. Shall we?"

With a nod, she accepted his arm and stepped toward his car. Thunder rumbled in the distance. With a tiny squeal, Belle nearly jumped into his arms. He could feel her shivering arms under his own. A moment later, she peeled herself out of his embrace and blushed.

Looking up from under long dark lashes, she apologized. "Sorry, Mitch. I've reacted poorly to thunder since childhood. It's a long story, but… thanks."

He opened the car door for her and smiled. "My pleasure. Lately, I jump at everything. Glad I could be of service for a change." She placed her hand on his arm and met his eyes.

"I've noticed small changes since you returned from your time embedded with the troops. I'm sure terrible does not describe all you experienced."

The innocence in her doe-like baby browns melted his heart. He didn't want to talk about it… ever, but if he opened his heart just a crack, maybe some of that gentle comfort she carried in spades might rub off.

Remaining silent as he rounded his Jeep, he slipped into the driver's seat and turned over the ignition. Pulling into traffic, he chanced a glance Isabella's way. She sat calmly enjoying the rain, not pushing him in any way. It's one of the things he noticed from the beginning… her air of peace.

He cleared his throat; she turned and smiled all the way to her eyes. "Thank you for this night out, Mitch," she beamed. "It's a real treat."

He nodded cautiously. "I'm not trying to avoid your statement, Isabella. Well… perhaps a little bit. I just haven't spoken about my time overseas. I don't know what to say exactly, but you're right. I've changed. Some changes I like, some I don't. There are moments in time that I wish I could make sense of, you know?"

When she reached over and squeezed his hand, the crack in the armor of his heart widened a fraction more to let the light of peace shine on the fear and darkness. A sensation of warmth spread through his body, and he squeezed her hand in return.

"Aren't you excited for tonight? The game promises to be a real nail biter!" Her laughter rang out like silver bells and just like that joy filled the car. His choice turned out well.

"Absolutely!" He cocked his head and gave her a curious look before turning into the concrete, multi-layered parking garage. "What's your favorite part of the game, Bella?"

Dark brown eyes twinkled in the pale fluorescent light. Bella bit her lip and chuckled.

"You won't believe me," she tossed her long, silky locks over her shoulder as she shook her head.

Pulling into a parking spot, he put the car in park and set the brake before turning. "Try me," he grinned obnoxiously.

"You asked… I like when the hockey players get into an argument and go off all halfcocked," the corner of her lips curved in a grin. She laughed at his surprise.

"Most of my life is very controlled, Mitch. Don't you sometimes wish you could just let everything go and come out swinging?" She lifted the back of her hand to her forehead and sighed with flair. "But alas, if I came out swinging, I'd probably end up decked out on the floor, so I watch other people do it. I like football for the same reason. You can yell at the T.V. all you want and no one gets hurt by your frustration." She shrugged with a grin. "It's good therapy."

He rubbed his jaw and grinned sheepishly. "Having been one who came out swinging in the past, I do not recommend the activity for the previously mentioned reason. I can get you a punching bag…?" he added with a wink.

She playfully punched his shoulder and marched toward the gate leaving him wondering at the unexplored depths of the woman he casually invited to a hockey game.

~

The roar of the crowd as the Royals scored the first point added to the roar in her heart and mind.

For a long time, her admiration of Mitch and his seemingly carefree attitude toward life sparked her own longing to be carefree. Her desire to be part of restoring his joy was working better than imagined.

She glanced over in time to see him shoving the last bite of chili dog in his mouth. He fist-pumped the air as the home team drove the puck past the opposing team's goalie for the winning point. When Mitch turned to hug her in a spontaneous, celebratory moment, she hugged him back for one glorious moment. The noise of the crowd grew louder. Mitch released her and joined in the melee. She smiled.

"You need a small snack before we go for dinner later," the serious war- correspondent came out all business, taking care of her every need. "What may I get you? I promised an evening on me, remember?"

Isabella bit her lip to hold in the joy at receiving Mitch's full focus. "A salted pretzel, please with cheese, not mustard. Thank you, Mitch," she whispered gently.

He nodded. "And what to drink?"

"Well…"

"Out with it, mi Bella. Tonight, you are my guest. No holding back on me."

She met his dark eyes. "In that case, a vanilla coke is my absolute favorite, but if they don't have it, Dr. Pepper will do."

"You got it. Be right back."

Normally inside her private box, she missed the excitement of being in the midst of the fans. The chili dogs tasted better than the gourmet offerings usually at her disposal. She smiled remembering the look on Caitlyn's face when the company box tickets arrived. The joy of giving filled her heart. Truth be told, she received the better end of the bargain tonight. The anonymity of being the newspaper administrative assistant served her well. No one suspected her true identity, and that's how she wanted it… for now.

Mitch didn't know how close he danced to the truth in alluding to her reticence in sharing personal information. Tonight, she risked being uncovered, but the moment superseded any concern. A shout escaped her lips. For once, she cut loose and joined the celebration. Tonight, she was just a girl from the paper, and Mitch… her co-worker, remained the guy she admired from a distance forever.

His seats were amazing, right behind the penalty box. Twenty minutes later, he returned, pretzel and a large drink in hand. He settled in when a cameraman focused on them. The "kiss cam" caught them on screen. Her eyes widened. Would he see? Would anyone recognize her? She saw the moment Mitch noticed the screen. He turned and raised an eyebrow in question. How did a girl answer such an unspoken query from a guy she only dreamed about? She answered with a little grin and a shrug. Let him interpret the smile as he will.

He did… and pressed his lips with reverence to her forehead. Respect and disappoint battled for position. Respect won out. She smiled up at him. He winked and squeezed her hand.

"What did I miss?" his eyes scanned the scoreboard and breathed a sigh of relief. The score remained unchanged. Back and forth the puck flew across the ice, each team blocking and retrieving in a nail-biting stalemate. The second half didn't disappoint with the two teams duking it out to finish with a 3-2 win!

Mitch motioned to the vender selling pendants for the Royals.

He forked over the cash and the man shoved a purple and gold pendant his way and shuffled down the concrete steps calling out his wares. Lips curled in a quirky grin, Mitch turned and handed the souvenir to her amidst the roar of the crowd.

"To remember the evening," he shouted. She beamed at his thoughtfulness and pressed the pendant close to her jersey. Mitch's small gesture meant the world… a world money could not buy.

Reaching up, she touched his shoulder to snag his attention. He flinched and turned as if surprised by her touch.

"Thank you, Mitch. Awesome game! And you're right... this is *so* much better than seeing the game alone."

He froze at her praise. Then suddenly, reminiscent of his former self, he snatched up her hand and pressed his lips to her slender fingers. "Hey, are you ready to get out of here before the rest of the crowd makes a beeline for the exits? I promised a dinner better than a pretzel," he raised questioning brown.

She nodded and gathering up her purse and jacket, followed him out the row. Once in the parking garage, he led her toward his dark green Jeep and opened the door. She breathed in the silence. The energy of the crowd rejuvenated and exhausted her. Mitch slid behind the wheel and pulled out just in time, Traffic began to form a line behind them. The sensation of relief spilled over them. Exchanging a knowing look, they chuckled together.

"Now, mi Bella, where may I take you to eat?" his baritone voice grew serious. "Do you have a favorite?"

She bit her lip. Among her peers, she would be scorned for her preference, but with Mitch… she felt safe enough, normal enough to take a risk.

"I know a tiny, whole-in-the-wall burger joint on 12th Street. I am famished for a good bacon-cheeseburger and fries," she admitted with a sheepish glance. "And maybe a cherry chip milkshake."

Mitch lifted his eyebrows. "Really, Isabella? Now you're talking! I took you for more of a salad kind of girl or maybe filet mignon. You are full of surprises tonight. A burger it is! Give me directions."

She complied. Christmas music wafted over the radio, and the stars twinkled to the music through the moon roof of the jeep. She sighed. The night begged to be remembered. In a busy office or a crowd full of fans, a person could still feel alone. Tonight, she shared a great evening and a tiny part of herself. The opportunity to share either rarely appeared. In attempting to bring Mitch's heart the gift of hope this Christmas, he gave her the gifts of comfort and joy. She leaned back into the seat and shut her eyes with a smile.

A hand reached over and squeezed her own. "You are a busy person, Isabella. I'm glad I could give you a night to relax. You deserve it. I see so much that you quietly give to others. Do you have someone in your life who takes care of you?"

Opening her eyes, she blinked back tears at his unexpected question. "Not for a long time, Mitch. I'm without family as well. The night you remember decorating cookies at my flat...? I needed friends around me. I lost my parents that year. I celebrated my first Christmas without them, so rather than curl up and cry, I decided to surround myself with joy." She chuckled and shot a meaningful look his way.

"I'd never made cookies before that evening. As experiments go, the night went pretty well; don't you think?"

He pulled into the parking lot of a small diner decked with Christmas lights and stopped the car before turning incredulous eyes her way. "You NEVER made cookies before that night? Isabella, they were homemade heaven. The atmosphere in the room felt like home. I didn't realize... I'm so sorry about your parents." He shook his head and squeezed her hand. "I would have liked to know. You appeared to have everything together that Christmas. I secretly admired you, your gift of hospitality, your hopefulness, your warmth."

He grinned. "I would have asked you out back then, but I thought you were SOOO out of my league. Thanks for coming with me tonight. To be honest, I didn't have the heart to go alone."

"What about Caitlyn? She would have gladly

come with you." She hoped the question behind the statement didn't uncover her true heart. He winked. She felt exposed.

"Yeah… but Caitlyn… she is like one of the guys. You aren't just using me for my tickets. I'd like to think that you wanted to come share the evening with me."

So, curiosity stirred behind both their words. He wanted her to *want* to be with him. "Mitch…"

"Yeah?"

"That Christmas in my apartment…?"

He raised an eyebrow and waited.

"I hoped you'd ask."

"No way!" He raised an incredulous eyebrow and shot his eyes her direction before glancing back at the road.

She felt her face redden with embarrassment and avoided his eyes.

"Ah man… I am totally kicking myself right now. Isabella…"

She ventured a glance.

"I can't redo the past, but… I'd like to continue to get to know you better. Would you take a chance on me this time? I'm… a bit broken right now. I see the negative in everything. I've lost hope in this crazy world and in people, and I'm not quite sure how to gain it back. If you're still interested…"

She rubbed his thumb. "I thought you'd never ask."

Chapter Four

Isabella arrived at the Newspaper office two hours before normal with a yawn. The night with Mitch left her humming Christmas carols even as a pile of work loomed on her desk. Stacks of paperwork awaiting the signature or approval of the "Boss" took up one whole corner of her administrative assistant desk. Two companies requesting to pull ads from the paper waited for her call, and a large prospective sponsor requested a face to face meeting.

She blew out a breath and got to work. Two hours later, the pile of work diminished significantly just as the office began to buzz with life. Mitch slipped into his office with a brief wave. Moments later, a cry of frustration burst forth from his direction. She hung up the phone and made her way to the star reporter's office with a memo from the boss.

Mitch's hands shook with her latest gift just delivered by the office mail.

"Mitch, what's wrong?"

He buried his head in his hands. "My gift giver has gone too far this time! I… I just can't!"

Concern shot through her heart. How could the donation of money and a request to see him at the soup kitchen cause such a reaction? She never dreamed... only hoped to remind him of his meaningful contribution in the past and renew his passionate gift of helping others. Where did she go wrong?

"What did the giver do wrong, Mitch?" she ventured.

Sorrowful eyes met her own. "I've seen too much pain, mi Bella... too much life without hope... too much despair. Nothing will change for these people. Every year, the same crowd shows up. We know each other by name... They could do so much, yet most don't want to try. Overseas... there is nothing but pain for the people I saw, and I can't do anything about the choices many of them make. The reality is overwhelming."

He buried his head in his hands to hide the emotion. Stepping forward, she removed the certificate from his hands and touched his shoulder.

"From the looks of it, the donation in your name has no requirements for you to show up personally... the request is just an added note saying those at the shelter miss you. The gift requires nothing from you, Mitch. You don't have to go down unless you really want to."

Rubbing his hands over his face, he straightened and cleared his throat. His baritone voice broke with raw emotion. "I told you I'm broken, Isabella. Everywhere I look, all I see is pain instead of peace; heartache in place of hope. Day after day, month after month, I remained positive that good change would come, hopeful that I could make a difference if I just got the story out, provided an extra meal, offered a kind word. Nothing mattered. Nothing changed. Well, one thing changed... me. Somewhere along the way, I lost hope, and I don't know how to get my optimism back."

He slumped down in his chair and shot her an irritated look. "I'm a real prize, huh. You should run while you have the chance. There are plenty of guys who'd love a shot with you, Mi Bella. I hear talk in the office pool all the time."

The sudden despair caught her off-guard. His hopelessness went deeper than she thought. *God, how do I help? Encourage him to get out of his despair and help anyway, or encourage him to take time to step back and regain his hope in you?*

Hope.

"Mitch, I need your help. The boss says we're to go to lunch, and I'm to bring you up to speed for a face to face with a large, potential donor."

Shock swept over him like a wave. "What! Why me, Isabella? I'm a war correspondent! What do I know about courting donors? In this mood, I'll probably scare them off!"

She handed him the memo, and he scanned the paper before handing the memo back.

"This doesn't explain why the boss asked for me. What do you know?"

"I can't say too much, Mitch, but my understanding is... changes are coming, and the boss sees you as a vital part of it. To be honest, I'm not that great at courting prospective investors or advertisers either. I'd be grateful for your help, and since it's on the boss, how about a great steak and baked potato? I'll even throw in the salad," she teased.

His brown eyes took on a merry twinkle. "Oh wow, a salad? I'm in." Sarcasm dripped from his lips. "Oh well, if the boss wants to live dangerously, who am I to stop it?"

She shrugged. "Eleven thirty?"

Mitch nodded as his only answer. She turned to leave; a bit shaken from the encounter. His voice, rough with emotion, stopped her.

"Isabella… thanks."

She turned and cocked her head. "For what?"

"For not pushing… for not trying to fix me… for just… listening."

A tight smile didn't quite meet her eyes, but she tried. The failure of her gift rocked her core. "Always, Mitch. I'm sorry about the gift. I'm certain the giver hoped to honor your past efforts and continue the work, but I'm sorry to hear the gift caused you pain."

He shook his head. "Thoughtful gestures are few and far between. I'm just not ready to get back out on the front lines, you know? Either overseas, or here at home, Someday perhaps. Just… thanks. See you at 11:30am!"

With a nod, she stepped out into the office pool of cubical and soaked up the gaudy garland and the attempt at a Christmas tree happening in the corner. Worrying would only zap her strength and accomplish nothing, so… she picked up a piece of mistletoe laying amidst the box of decoration and tacked the small decoration to the breakroom doorway. She allowed laughter to bubble forth. Watching who got stuck under the mistletoe would be a fun pastime since she could see the action from her desk. Choosing joy… choosing hopeful moments… *the joy of the Lord is my strength*, she smiled.

God, this Christmas season and all year long… You are good. You give reason to hope. With a melody of hope in her heart, she made her way back to her desk.

A crimson poinsettia sat on her desk, delivered by a local florist. She snatched up the card… and blushed.

Thanks for brightening my evening like you brighten the office every day.

~Mitch

A joyful exclamation from the doorway echoed as Caitlyn hurried to her desk chattering like a magpie as she stepped up to Isabella's desk and planted both hands flat on the desk.

"Alright Bella, dish up the info! Who is my amazing Secret Santa? Did you orchestrate this? Only you could make something of this magnitude happen. Someone went through you. I just know, so spill, girl!"

She paused to catch a breath and noticed the flowers for the first time. "Oh… someone has an admirer! Who is the lucky guy?" She reached for the card, but Bella snatched the card up first with a mischievous grin.

"Somethings, like a Secret Santa and Secret admirers, are meant to be *Seeecrets,* Caitlyn, oh great reporter! You'll get nothing out of me! Now…

shoo! Don't you have some story to break or a criminal to bust?"

The redhead wagged her finger and stepped away. "Don't think you are getting away that easily, my friend. I'll figure everything out! Wait and see!"

Time flew by and soon eleven thirty arrived.

~

Adeline brushed her heavy, dark curls over her shoulder and pondered what to do next. People watching elevated her reporting. Information often came to the patient watcher, but now, something didn't add up. She'd been out of the office too much to notice the changes before, but the boss rarely, if ever, showed his face anymore. Yesterday, she placed a couple of request forms on his assistant's desk as a test.

Leaning back in her chair, she bit her lip and held a last year's Christmas card to the light next to the signed request form. They didn't match. She watched as Isabella entered the boss' office. Rising from her chair, she casually walked over to the door and dropped a paper. Stooping to pick the item up, she paused to listen, and heard voices. When did the boss come in? Footsteps sounded. She snatched up her paper, and casually moved next to Isabella's administrative desk.

The door opened, and Isabella stepped out with a smile.

"Good morning, Adeline. How may I assist you?"

Addie strained her neck to see past the closing

door. "Is the boss in? I'd really like to discuss a matter with him. I haven't seen him in ages." Did she imagine the reaction or did Isabella pale just a little?

Isabella adjusted her black, wireframe glasses. "The boss unavailable these next couple of weeks, Adeline. Is your request urgent? Perhaps, I could convey a message."

Addie tilted her head in concern. "Isabella, I get the idea that you are hiding something. No one has seen the boss... almost all year. Am I the only one asking questions? What's going on?"

Isabella smiled. "No, absolutely, its okay to ask questions, Adeline. Since the owner's passing last year, things have been a bit unconventional, but I understand on good authority that all will be made right at the Christmas party. No jobs are in jeopardy. Good things are coming. I know things seem unsettling right now, but I've been assured that everything is about to move forward with a great future for the paper. Just be patient a little while longer, okay? By the way, how's your Secret Santa treating you?"

Shaking her finger, Addie grinned. "I see what you are trying to do, Isabella, by changing the subject, but I'll wait... until the party and no longer. As for my Secret Santa? He's got good taste in literature. A signed copy of a new release I hoped for showed up on my desk just this morning. Until the Christmas party then..."

Isabella's lips curled into a smile that reached her eyes. "Until the party.

~

Mitch sat at his already clean desk and stared at an international headline. Reporters in his niche alternated between front line reporting and writing perspective on events for the folks back home. Either way, the job felt like always waiting for something bad to happen.

He picked up a shell from the Mediterranean and turned the small piece of God's creation over in his hand. The spiral beauty, the soft white and apricot coloring combined with mother-of-pearl inside to create a soothing effect. He'd found the shell during a brief moment of R & R between assignments one weekend in Greece. God's goodness to give relief just when he needed restoration, never failed, and he definitely needed restoring now.

He couldn't believe a simple donation to his favorite shelter and the mention of his absence caused him to fall apart. Perhaps a visit in the future just to say hi might hurry his healing.

He smiled. Isabella refreshed his soul. He checked his watch. Time to say a prayer for renewal and take a girl to lunch. Today… he counted his blessings. They were many. Isabella gave so much and expected little in return. Hope sprouted to do likewise. He rubbed his hands together in delight. As soon as the lunch meeting ended, he would get to work on his office Secret Santa projects.

He stepped out of his office in time to see Caitlyn wag her finger and walk away from Isabella's desk. He'd heard her boasting all morning about the greatness of her Secret Santa's gift, even popping into his office to compare notes about the game. Shifting through the cubicles, he made his way toward Isabella's desk.

He stopped at Adeline's desk to hand off a copy of an email from a Parisian source and lifted a brow at finding her nose in the novel he left this morning. She mentioned the series on her paper, and he knew the author. He prided himself in the gift since the idea sparked. Adeline barely glanced up, motioned for him to drop the paper on her desk. He chuckled.

Out of the corner of his eye, Isabella moved the poinsettia he sent to the most prominent place in her office. The small action unwrinkled a corner of the noble character he stashed deep inside his heart. Someone valued his gesture. Though a tiny thing in the grand scheme of life, actions mattered.

He moved toward her office, stopped in the doorway and tapped on the white casing. When she glanced up, her eyes brightened. She checked her watch and gathered her phone and purse.

"Wow, this morning has flown by. I'm so grateful for your presence during this meeting. I'm really nervous. I prepared a file for you to read on the way to lunch."

Reaching out to accept the manila folder she offered, their hands touched. Sparks flew. She dropped her purse. He dropped the file. Numerous apologies filled the air as he bent to gather the fallen items only to knock her purse out of her hand and drop his file again. He tried again. This time, she bumped his head with her own.

Laughing, he straightened.

"How about we try this one more time, Mi Bella. I'll gather both things. You are perfect right where you are," he grinned. A beautiful blush bloomed on her fair skin. He ducked to hide his pleasure.

For a being such a dismal guy at the beginning of the month, reconnecting with Isabella tapped back into his brighter personality. His once carefree nature blossomed in her presence.

Gathering her purse, phone and his folder, he stood and handed a suddenly shy Isabella her items and nodded toward the door.

"After you, my lady," he tipped his head in a slight bow, and her blush deepened. Rosy, full lips curled in a smile meant for him alone and made his heart glad as he followed her toward the parking garage.

Speaking over her shoulder, Isabella shot him a question snapping him out of his haze. "Do you mind if I drive? That way you can study the file as we go?"

"Not a problem. Lead the way. I believe you promised a steak…"

The merry sound of light laughter cheered the dismal concrete garage. "Yes, I did. Red meat just for you. I'm the red…"

He halted in his tracks and stared. "No way, Izzy. You drive a Jeep too?" He could hear the shock in his own voice. *What gives about this girl, God?*

He could have sworn she enjoyed the upscale life. Though briefly displaying a different side the night of the game, today, as usual, her golden-brown hair rested in a bun at the nape of her neck. Black rimmed glasses graced her slender nose adding to her conservative, non-adventurous look.

A Jeep? Really? What other surprises hid behind the soft exterior?

She beamed back at him behind the glasses. "She's my pride and joy. I bought her because when I go rock-climbing, I get into some pretty serious back country. Hop in and let's go get that steak."

Okay… after he picked his jaw off the floor, he managed to climb into the passenger side of the jeep and pretend to open the folder. Did his prim secretary just confess to buying an all-terrain vehicle for her rock-climbing?

Forcing his eyes to focus on the prospective, client profile, he forced. all thoughts of the intriguing woman driving aside. He glanced up concerned as they pulled into the parking lot of an exclusive quiet club known for its steaks.

He turned in his seat as she parked the car. "Isabella, you're just getting this profile to me *now?* This company potentially brings half a million in annual advertising if you add both newspaper and radio ads! A meeting of this magnitude requires *weeks* of research and preparation! What is going on?"

She ducked her head. "This client contacted us two days ago having just dropped our competitor after the company made some immoral decisions that conflict with this client's standards. They want to transfer *all* their business to us the first of January if we can assure them of our ethical standards and family values."

Stunned, Mitch sat back in his seat. "Why isn't the boss handling a client of this magnitude? Why leave the details to you and me?"

Isabella bit her lip and pushed her glasses up on her nose again out of nervous habit. "The answer is simple, but I've been asked not to share much until the Christmas party. I *can* tell you a couple of things. The board watches its top contributors, and they've noticed two things about you, Mitch. First, you're the best they have, but you're tired. Second, since the owner passed away, there has been a leadership vacuum. They want you to fill it.

When the opportunity to land this client came up, you were tasked to land it. I'm authorized to tell you that if you land this account, the position of Editor-in-Chief will be offered for your consideration."

Mitch clutched the folder like a life-line and struggled between panic and relief. His time on the frontlines wore him down, but could he really do the job of Editor-in-Chief? Following Isabella into the softly lit restaurant, he prayed.

God, the idea of this change brings such relief. Is this Your plan? Please direct my steps, renew my heart, and lead me into paths of righteousness for Your Name's sake.

Peace came, along with the steaks Isabella ordered. He mouthed his thanks. Isabella reached across the table and squeezed his hand. The human contact helped.

"God's got you, Mitch. Let His joy fill your heart. You've served Him well for so long. Don't give up the fight, just direct others to join in alongside. Now, dig in and enjoy a taste of good gifts. These filets are amazing!"

"Ah ha! I knew you were a filet mignon type of girl!"

A startled look crossed her face. "Of course… I guess I look at myself as a *red meat* kind of girl. Burgers, filets, if its meat… I'll eat it."

"A woman after my own heart. Shall we thank God for this bounty and ask for His help today?" Instantly, she bowed her head offering one more example of her worth… more than gold.

Raising his head from the prayer, Mitch squeezed Isabella's hand, and dug into his loaded baked potato. Exchanging details about the client and discussing various approaches took up most of the meal. Swallowing the last bite of filet, Mitch wiped his mouth with the linen napkin and lay it beside his plate.

"I think we are as ready as we can be on short notice, Isabella. Please let the board know I appreciate the opportunity. The thought of continuing as a war correspondent weighs heavy on me lately. Editor-in-Chief seems a huge task, but one I would definitely be honored to consider if the board thinks I'm a fit."

Isabella signed the bill after using the company card, and they headed toward the door. Reaching the parking lot, Mitch couldn't hold his curiosity in any longer.

"So… I have to ask? Rock-climbing? Would you like to climb together sometime? I know this great climbing gym nearby. My normal favorite site is under snow right now."

Isabella stuck the keys in the ignition and paused before turning the engine over. Twisting to face him, she studied him for a moment before answering.

"Mitch, at the risk of sounding forward, there is a reason for my next question. I'll explain depending on your answer. Are we spending time together as co-workers and friends or do you hope for something more in our future?"

Mitch rubbed a hand over his developing five o'clock shadow. Wow, Bella didn't pull punches. Did he know his own heart? Isabella brought out the best in him. What did he have to offer in return? For just a moment, his carefree nature reemerged. Whether she wanted him or felt he offered anything, she could decide. He knew he wanted a shot at getting to know her… at considering if she fit as a future mate… Whoa… marriage? His heart pounded out affirmation and jumped ship right into the hands of the woman before him. He cleared his throat and took her hand.

"Isabella, I've always admired you, but in these last couple of weeks, I *need* to know you better. I can't really explain it, but I want more of you. Even in my carefree days, I've never been a player. I enjoy people, but I've rarely dated. With you… I'd like to see if we have a future."

He shrugged his shoulders and ran his hand over his face again. "Wow, I've never said anything quite like that before." He ventured a glance her direction. "How'd I do?"

She turned the ignition over with a shy smile. "I'd love to go rock climbing with you, Mitch. I don't want us to be late. I'll explain my forthrightness later, but I since you want to get to know more of me, I have just the opportunity on Friday. Do you have a tux?"

"I'll have to dust the thing off, but for you… anything."

Her laughter rang like silver bells. "Friday, meet at my place at six thirty pm, dressed to the nines. Then Saturday, I'll make it up to you and go rock-climbing?" Her soft soprano wobbled with first sound of insecurity. Somehow that knowledge sooth his nerves.

He winked at her. "Planning our next two dates, huh. Afraid I won't show for the second one?" he teased.

Isabella visibly winced. "Something like that, Mitch. Promise you'll still go rock-climbing after you get a glimpse of who I am? This is where I usually don't get a call back. I want to know you better as well. I enjoy your company."

He squeezed her hand. "Promise. We will do your gig Friday and mine Saturday and go from there, okay?"

Nodding, she squeezed back. Five minutes later, they pulled into the parking lot of a major craft distributor. Mitch glanced her way. Isabella turned all business, but he could see a sliver of nervousness in her eyes.

"Let's pray, Mi Bella. Shall we? Father God, we trust you to direct our steps and give us the words to say today. We desire to honor you both in business and in our budding relationship. We're trusting you to lead us. In the Name of Jesus Christ, Amen."

The light of peace filled her eyes. "Thanks, Mitch. You take the lead on this as our prospective Editor-in-Chief, okay? I'm your administrative assistant."

He grinned. "The boss dating the help, huh… I've heard it's rather frowned upon. Sounds like living dangerously," he teased.

She tilted her head, and her eyes sparkled he stepped out of the car. "You have no idea," he thought heard her whisper.

Chapter Five

Isabella smiled in all the right places, interjected a few facts about the company and occasionally nudged Mitch under the table and passed him a hand-written note with an idea. The intensity fostered on the battlefield adapted and refocused to meet the corporate arena head on. In the end, Mitch's integrity, intensity, and determination to win won over the client wholeheartedly.

She knew her own strengths, and they were many; yet she also understood her limitations. Even through a tough year, Mitch belonged in this world. The company CEO stood and shook Mitch's hand signaling the meeting's close. Laughter and the talk of a casual meeting of golf or racquetball sealed a corporate friendship in making.

For a moment, she allowed herself to dream. Could she have finally found a man who would fit in her world? The thought of Mitch in a tuxedo brought the blood rushing to her cheeks again. Suddenly, she heard the CEO mention her name. She glanced up embarrassed at having been caught wool-gathering. Mitch winked.

"I told Andrew that I am doubly blessed," his

face lit with a mischievous grin. "Not only are you the best asset the company has, but you are a gift to me as well. He mentioned that he and his lovely wife look forward to seeing us at the Christmas Gala for the hospital fundraiser Friday." He reached for her, and she stepped forward to take his outreached hand and turned toward their new client.

"I would be delighted to meet your wife," she smiled.

He nodded toward Mitch as a board member snagged the man. "We met last year, Lady Marion, or is it, Isabella?"

Isabella felt her knees go weak. "My full name is Isabella Marionette Frias Goldberg. "At the company I'm Isabella Frias, an omission, but still the truth. Before my father passed, I came on board as his administrative assistant to learn the business. I've never wanted the Editor-in-Chief role, but we couldn't find the right person. The board suggested I continue on in my role until the right person came along. It's been a heavy load, but I think we hit gold with Mr. Torres."

"As do I," Andrew replied. "I have been impressed by you… and your father last year. I am so sorry to hear about his passing. You've done an admirable job. I've been watching, but I know the burdens of running a company." He tilted his head in thought before adding,

"Mr. Torres… doesn't know the full extent of who you are yet does he?"

She bit her lip and shot a nervous glance in Mitch's direction. "When Mitch return stateside, I knew… he is born for the role of Editor-in-Chief.

Somehow, working together, our hearts got involved. I told him there is more to me than meets the eye, so I asked him to attend with me Friday in order to reveal the full truth."

Pensive, Andrew nodded and shook his head. "If I were you, I'd tell him today. I look forward to partnering with your company, Isabella Marion," he winked. "Good day."

Stepping into the light of day, Isabella pondered the CEO's thoughts. Since Andrew revealed the event she asked Mitch to attend, why not tell him now? The very thought shook her to her core. Every time she reached this level in a relationship, the guy got cold feet, overwhelmed or whatever and bailed on her. What if Mitch could not handle being in a relationship with the owner of a media conglomerate?

She sucked in a breath as she pushed the key fob to unlock her Jeep. Anonymity allowed her to drive her own car, live a normal life. Taking a risk made for a fearful endeavor, but joy waited on the other side if Mitch completely accepted her. Her heart pounded in her chest. Mitch slid into the passenger seat and studied her with concern.

"Mi Bella, this is a victory. You look like you're at a wake. What's wrong? Did my comment about our relationship seem out of place? The man could tell I have eyes for you…"

Isabella shook her head. "No, Mitch. Would you mind if we grab a shake and take a moment to walk at the park before heading back to the office? I planned to share something important with you Friday night, but now… I'd rather bend your ear if you don't mind. I'm nervous, and I need to hear your heart."

Concern wrinkled his brow. "Of course, I'm all yours."

Moments later, they pulled into the park, two chocolate malts in hand. Crazy! They even ordered the same drink! Mitch opened her door for her, and grabbing her hand, led her to a bench. Using his black winter gloves, he dusted off the snow and bowed.

"Your seat... seriously Mi Bella. What's on your mind? I find things work better when we just spit them out. Whatever the issue is, we'll handle the challenges together."

She pulled her red wool pea coat close and shook her head wishing her hair draped down today. "You say that now, Mitch, and I hope it's true. Experience dies hard." She patted the seat beside her and paused to study a couple of squirrels angrily quarreling over a nut. She pointed them out and chuckled.

"See there... even squirrels get greedy. People change when wealth is involved, Mitch." She turned to face him. "So, I'll take your advice and jump in... I'm your boss, Mitch. I own the media syndicate that you work for. I've been my own administrative assistant for the past year since my father died. I started out working for my father to learn the business, but when he died unexpectedly, the board recommended I stay on until a new Editor-in-Chief could be found." Then you... we..." she buried her head in her hands.

Suddenly, she felt his strong hands tug on her.

Lifting anxious eyes, she met his studious browns. He raised a dark eyebrow.

"Isabella, so at this point in past relationships, let me guess… the guy either got greedy or caved."

She sucked in a steadying breath. "That about sums everything up. And you, Mitch?"

His eyes swept her face with curiosity. "I'm full of questions, like: do you really need these glasses?" He slid them off her face. She grinned and shook her head.

"Hmm… so the studious, librarian look… also part of the disguise?" Again, she nodded as he pulled the pins from her bun and set free her long, golden brown locks. The warmth of having her hair down could not match the warmth growing in her heart. She felt so good.

The kindness in Mitch's smile filled her heart. "Now, what else…? Hmm, how about your name?" He grew suddenly serious. "Are you really Isabella Frias? I believed the owner's name to be Goldberg?" he questioned.

She bit her lip. "My full name is Isabella Marionette Frias-Goldberg. Social circles know me as Marion Goldberg, but at the office I've always been Isabella. My father suggested I use my mother's name at work, so I would not receive special treatment."

He pulled away, and she felt the loss of his warmth.

"So, wait… It's you who forced me to participate in the Secret Santa game this year?" His voice grew cool. "Why?"

"For the very reason mentioned in the memo I

sent." She sighed and folded her hands in her lap to still the shaking. "I'd presented your name to the board for Editor-In-Chief, Mitch, but I knew… it's been a tough season. You were spiraling, and the board's concerns about your interaction with employees began to gain traction. I regrouped and quietly forced you out of your comfort zone. I truly believe you are the man for the job, but the board has a say."

"And today…?" he questioned and began to pace, leaving a mess of footprints in the snow.

"This client changes the outlook for the company moving forward. Advocating for my own company is difficult for me. I'm better behind the scenes. Carrying the whole load this last year…" She sighed and shook off the heaviness of the load, choosing instead to turn a bright smile on the man before her.

"Mitch, your innovation, passion and integrity sealed the deal today. When the chairman of the board texted asking for an update, I told him you nailed the meeting and even encouraged the client to go with a larger package… In five minutes, I received a follow-up text. The job of Editor-in-Chief is yours if you want it. Please take it… even… even if you don't take me."

His cold silence stabbed her in the heart. Patience demanded she allow him time to absorb and process the information. She forced her lips to remain silent as he stood, rubbed his jaw and turned to look up at the squirrels.

Her heart pounded out the moments, waiting…

He turned and warily looked her over. "This

thing between you and I... are you for real or 'courting the prospective editor'?"

She wanted to hug him for the question. Instead, she stood and stepped beside him. He took a step back. She bit her lip and started to reach for his hand, but paused. She would not chase him.

"It's so *very* real, Mitch. I've held you in my heart since cookie-making. When I suggested you as Editor-in-Chief, I *never* dreamed you would remember or notice me. I gave up *my* box seats to the game for Caitlyn, so that I could go with you. By the way, thank you for asking."

"Box seats, huh..." He chuckled and shook his head. "You owned *box seats* to the game that night and gave them up to go with me?"

"Box seats are nothing if you're in them alone, Mitch. You offered me something that money and power are impotent to give... friendship, connection, hope."

His eyes twinkled "Just where would you like to see our relationship go, Isabella?"

She couldn't help the tears. "Forward... definitely forward. I truly long for a knight in shining armor. I've played the part of the superwoman who has everything: money, power, career, but I long for: rock-climbing, cheeseburgers, hockey games, and someday a husband and family. I never intended to deceive. I just have to be careful, Mitch."

A light went on in his head; she could see the wheels turning. "Friday... you were going to show me your world Friday, while making me promise to keep a Saturday date as well. Afraid I'll run?"

She grinned, "Just hedging my bets…"

He touched his forehead to hers as snow began to fall. He chuckled and pulled her close. "Well, my lady, we have two dates left at least. Let's see where we go from there, okay?"

He wiped her tears with his thumb and kissed her forehead. "Besides, didn't I just get a promotion to being *your* boss in a weird sort of way? Depending on the situation, how about we alternate for now," he winked.

She giggled. "Dating the 'boss'… quite convoluted isn't it!" She lay her head on his chest. "Mitch…"

He set his chin on the crown of her head. "Yeah…?"

"Thanks for not bailing and at least hearing me out."

He pulled back and sobered. "To be honest, all kinds of crazy thoughts swirl in my overactive mind right now. Some great, some not so great, but I choose to take them one at a time. No more secrets between us, okay?"

Isabella bit her lip and pondered the Secret Santa reveal. Wincing, she turned hopeful eyes on her 'prince among men'. "Would you allow me just one more secret? It's nothing earth-shattering. Just a Christmas surprise…?"

Mitch shook his head and rubbed the back of his hair. "Woman, you sure do push a man to the very edge. The thing is…" his eyes sparkled. "The fall offers a thrill I can't seem to pass up. Go ahead. Have your secret!"

"Race you to the car?" she giggled and began to

run hoping he would chase. He did. Joy filled her heart.

Chapter Six

Mitch knew he should be intimidated by the wealth and power at the venue tonight, yet all he could think about… Isabella unleashed, unhindered, unfettered. The traditional glasses, the bun at the nape of the neck, and pants suits daily masked something more. Hints of her true personality shone just beneath the surface; he couldn't wait to dive deeper. With his Jeep buffed and polished in anticipation of the evening, he stood nervously at her doorstep. Mitch adjusted his tie, knocked and waited.

A vision in shimmering emerald green opened the door. The door jam proved a solid way to steady himself. Long golden-brown curls spilled freely down Isabella's back. Emeralds sparkled at her ears and graced her slender neck. High heels accentuated her long legs and a dress that looked like a mermaid tail graced a lovely figure.

Gone were the black glasses. Eyes more green than brown demurred under long dark lashes. Speechless, he handed her the bird of paradise bouquet purchased with the intent to impress. Nothing compared with the way Isabella looked at him. Opening the door wider with a smile, in a graceful, sweeping motion she beckoned for him to enter.

"These are lovely, Mitchell, how exotic and thoughtful. The car will be here in a moment. Please, have a seat while I put these lovely blooms in water."

Still in a daze, he did as instructed until her words hit. "Car? I assumed we'd be taking mine. It's clean and polished."

"I told you tonight would show you my world. I drive my Jeep because I refuse the car provided for me on regular days, but on nights like tonight... Sanders would have my head. You are my guest tonight, Mitch. Please, just enjoy the flash and privileges and don't let anything intimidate you, okay? Money and power are tools to be used to help the helpless, and I've discovered that I can be responsible, charitable and still enjoy the fruits of hard work and God's blessing."

Stretching her slender arm, she reached for his hand. Enjoy the evening with me tonight, okay?"

He nodded and grinned. "Aside from my dropped jaw, which I left on your front step, did I tell you that you look beautiful tonight?"

Her eyelids fluttered with shy grace at his compliment. Her ruby lips curled in a smile of delight.

"And you, Sir, look dashing in your tuxedo, rugged five o'clock shadow and elegant watch. I am proud to be seen with you tonight. Thank you for agreeing to come." Her phone chimed with an alert. She nodded toward the door. "The car is here. Shall we?"

Mitch stood and offered his arm. Isabella snagged her delicate purse and slipped her hand in the crook of his arm. After stepping through the door, he halted. "What should I call you tonight, Mi Bella?"

She winced at the reminder. "You could call me Isabella, but this crowd knows me as Marion or Marionette. I will leave the decision to you. I like when you call me Isabella. I feel more like myself, but…" she hesitated. Sensing her discomfort, he stepped in and placed his hand over the one in the crook of his arm.

"Tonight, you are Lady Marion and I am Robin Hood," he bowed.

She giggled as he opened the door for her. "Thank you, Sir Robin," she whispered her gratitude.

The gala event impressed. Chandeliers sparkled, casting prisms of light. Andrew Bower approached with a blond lady in a slender, elegant black gown. Bowing over Isabella's hand, he smiled and turned to introduce the lady with him.

"Wonderful to see you again, Marion and Mitchell. May I introduce my lovely wife Karen? Darling, this is Marion, President of Awe Star Media. Mitch is her new Editor-in-Chief."

The gracious older woman extended her hand in greeting as a smile tipped her lips. "It's wonderful to meet you both. Andrew came home very impressed by your meeting. Thank you for attending the hospital fundraiser tonight."

Andrew's blue eyes were for his wife alone.

"Karen, you've out done yourself with the gala this year."

Turning his glance back their direction, he grinned. "Thirty-five years and I'm her biggest fan."

Karen beamed. "Enjoy yourselves and give generously," she cajoled before turning to another couple.

The entire ball room glistened with midnight blue silk and sparkling light of candles and chandeliers. One end of the room, tables laden with silent auction items beckoned the generous. On the other end, a buffet unlike any other, lay spread for a King, and in the center, against the wall set a live reproduction of the manger, reminding everyone of the true King of Kings. Overhead, a lovely banner announcing the Silent Night Auction & Gala pronounced the event's true purpose.

Mitch leaned in close as they made their way along the silent auction tables. "You are the loveliest lady in the room, Lady Marion…" Purpose accomplished. She blushed. After bidding on a child's painting of a sailboat and an evening for two at an exclusive restaurant in town, he whispered.

"I am famished, Mi Bella and the King's feast is calling. Do you suppose we could head that direction?

Lashes fluttering, she snickered behind her hand. "Far be it from me to allow Sir Robin to starve." Slipping her hand in the crook of his arm, she followed his lead to the table and then to a small nook set with tiny tables and chairs. Once seated, she leaned in close.

"Watch out, here comes our most challenging share-holder, Eliza Pumpernickel. She's the sister of father's oldest friend and partner… and always resented my mother. Last year, she inherited her brother's shares. Now, she likes to flex her muscles just to prove she wields some power," she whispered through a smile.

"And does she?" He whispered back as a sharp-edged woman forced her way toward them through the crowd.

"Third largest share-holder after myself and my father's silent partner," she answered out of the corner of her mouth and extended a hand in greeting as the woman in question approached with a frown wrinkling her brow.

"Marionette, darling, I'm simply famished," Eliza raised a hand to her brow and plopped into a chair at their table. "Fetch me a plate before I faint."

Isabella moved to comply when Mitch placed a steady hand on her knee under the table. "Good evening, Ms.… I'm sorry, I don't believe we've been introduced."

Startled, the unpleasant woman turned her head and acknowledged Mitch for the first time. Scanning him up and down as if for flaws, she waved him off and turned back to Isabella. "Now dear, about my plate…"

Mitch rose to his feet and pulled Isabella with him. "My apologies, Ma'am, but this is our dance. If you'd like, I'd be happy to send one of the wait-staff your way…"

Tugging Isabella toward the dance floor, he bowed to the disgruntled older woman.

Once on the floor, he pulled a speechless Isabella into his arms and began to lead them in a waltz. She fit perfectly in his arms. A couple of weeks ago, his heart scoffed at the world, shook from the inside and wanted to hide. Suddenly, with this woman in his life, he found new purpose, new joy. *Thank you, Heavenly Father, for the timing of this hope. I felt tapped out, lost… but You never left me alone. Just… thank you.*

Turning his partner to the music, he caught a look of awe on her face. *So… maybe she's feeling this connection as well.* He caught her again and smiled as their eyes met. Her hand settled on his shoulder before she shook her head and spoke,

"Mitch, you seem to have come to life this week. The effect is stunning. You amazed Andrew Bower, our prospective client, put old Eliza politely in her place, and seem to be adjusting to this other world of which I am part." A small breath left her lips. "I let you see both sides to my life," Isabella bit her lip in nervous thought. "Are we still on for rock-climbing?"

He leaned in close and took her hand, "You know… in history and legend, Lady Marion lived as ward of the King. Impressive… just like this gala and your beautiful gown. However, perhaps you forget, Mi Bella, that in history, Isabella *reigned* as queen, much higher than a ward of the court. In my heart and mind, though Marion is impressive, Isabella reigns, and I can't wait to see her rock-climb tomorrow."

He couldn't be certain in the soft light, but tears glistened in Isabella's eyes. "Be careful, Mitch…

you teeter on the verge of the romantic. Heroes are forged with lesser statements. Are you certain you want to lose your reputation as the office cynic?"

Raising one eyebrow, he paused and studied her face, taking his time. He rubbed a hand over his carefully crafted five-o'clock shadow. "Hmm… perhaps you could keep this newly acquired information to yourself. I'll spring for cheese fries tomorrow," he bribed, "Although, those goat-cheese, bacon-wrapped dates are amazing! Shall we take a break and grab a few. It seems our intruder found the buffet table all by herself," he teased.

He led her off the floor to the opposite side of the huge buffet from their unwanted friend. Snagging two plates, he handed one to Isabella and picked up a date to place on his plate.

To his surprise, Isabella snagged the morsel from his fingers and popped the bite into her mouth. "By the way… these are my favorite gourmet snack. You might want to take notes," she teased. He stared. Isabella… the prim and proper administrative assistant turned heiress just flirted back with him. She nodded toward the silent auction.

"I'm going to check our bids and up them if need be. Fill your plate," she smiled. "You've definitely earned it."

Two hours later, they headed home with a number of winning items, the voucher for the exclusive restaurant among his cache. When the limo pulled up to Isabella's flat, Mitch exited his side and jogged around to open the luxury car door. Offering his hand, he thrilled when she accepted and allowed him to help her from the vehicle. He walked her to the door. Upon reaching it, she turned toward him. He brushed a stray hair from her eyes and smiled.

"Thank you again for letting me into your world, Mi Bella." Bending at the waist, he gave a gallant bow and kissed the back of her hand. "Until tomorrow... I look forward to beating you to the top of the rock-climbing wall."

Pulling the hand he kissed to her chest, she sucked in a breath and blinked. "Last one to the top buys the burgers?" Her eyes sparkled like the emeralds at her ears and throat taking his breath away even amidst the playful banter. The layers to this lovely woman continued to surprise him. What would tomorrow reveal? He couldn't wait to find out.

"You're on... Until tomorrow then... Good night, Mi Bella."

She blew him a kiss before slipping into her flat. He tossed the keys to his Jeep into the air and caught them with one hand behind his back. For the first time in years, he felt like whistling a tune. He glanced back over his shoulder and saw Isabella wave from her window. He waved back. *Until tomorrow...*

Chapter Seven

Rock climbing soothed the soul, gave problems to solve in real-time and a sense of accomplishment upon reaching the top. Since weather prohibited climbing in the best locations during December, Isabella arranged to meet Mitch at Three Strands Climbing Gym on the west side of town. Last night, Mitch proved his ability to handle the most egotistical board member with confident humility and a touch of humor, something she still needed to master.

Something switched between them. Mitch's despondent, defensive, wounded spirit vanished. In its place stood the man she knew existed all along: confident, strong, fearless in taking the lead, patient and talented. Showing up an hour early allowed her to process the change. Leadership looked amazing on him.

Reaching for a purple handhold, she hung onehanded for a moment in space until successfully swinging her mark. Two more feet, and she reached the top. For the next few minutes, she tackled the wall. Nothing else mattered. She tagged the top and made her way down in a couple of jumps. Snagging a bright red towel from her bag, she patted her face.

If Mitch stepped out in courage to lead the company, she could finally take a step back and breathe. Last night, donors and clients wanted to meet him, listen to his thoughts for the future of the company. She'd been keeping things together, holding on for this moment, and now hope beckoned.

She snagged her empty water bottle and headed for the water fountain. The cool water soothed her dry throat. Once filled, she tucked the bottle back in her bag and headed for the ladies' room to freshen up a bit for their "date". Christmas music played over the speakers throughout the gym. She glanced out the window at the gently falling snow. The forecast called for snow the rest of the afternoon.

She tidied up her ponytail, added a touch of lip gloss and body spray before heading back into the lobby. The snow fell heavier now. The door jingled open. The wind blew Mitch and a hundred snowflakes into the building. She laughed at his snowman like appearance.

"What...?" He moaned, dusting off the white flakes. "I feel like I scaled Mt. Everest just to get here!" He scanned her gym clothes with appreciation and grinned. "You must've arrived early."

"Guilty," she grinned. "We almost have the gym to ourselves. Everyone else wised up and bailed."

Tugging off his jacket, he shot her a reproving glance. "Then the adventure is passing them by. I prefer to say that we are blessed to have the place to ourselves."

Cocking her head, she stared at him. "What's changed, Mitch? Last month, I worried about you. You'd become this sullen, hopeless, irritable guy. Now… you're reminding me to stay focused on the positive." She elbowed him flirtatiously. "I like it."

Pulling on his climbing harness, he grinned. "I have a Secret Santa who apparently wants me to remember to keep the fairy tale alive… that dreams and hopes can come true. In my darkest moments, God keeps telling me to hope, and I have this amazing woman in my life. She inspires me. She brings hope to others and never quits."

He stepped closer and lifted her chin. "I'm here, Isabella. I've seen how you've carried the company and the employees this past year. I never realized the extent to which you carried everyone's burdens, but I'm here now. I'm strong. I can shoulder some of the burdens now. Ready for a climb?"

Isabella blew out a breath she didn't even know she held and nodded. Time to climb… as a team. Climbing didn't happen in a vacuum. One climbed, the other supported the rope. Trusting her rope to someone else felt amazing.

The snow fell; the climbs were magnificent; the company… like finding her soulmate. They paused for a water and energy bar break and stared at the falling snow.

Mitch squeezed her hand. "I think we'd better call things quits for now. I'll follow you home. Grab your bag and let's go. Agreed."

"I think you're right." She snatched up her things and met him by the Jeep. "Thanks, Mitch for a great day. See you at the office."

He nodded. "I'll see you home and wave you off. Until tomorrow, Mi Bella."

~

Arriving late to work the next morning, Isabella discovered a small nativity set and a batch of terrible looking homemade Christmas cookies. A card from Mitch simply read: reminding you of what's important. The gesture brought happy tears to her eyes. She grinned at the thought of what awaited him following his afternoon meeting with the board.

In truth, compared to the gifts others were giving and receiving, her gifts were getting a little out of hand, but helping him with his gifting as well as giving to him filled her own heart with joy.

Tying the last balloon and shoving it in a large garbage bag, she waited until the door to the conference room closed with Mitch safely in it and motioned to the mail guy to give her a hand with the three, full garbage bags. Thankfully, most of the office sat empty during lunch.

Isabella stepped into Mitch's office carrying a large pewter statue of St. George Slaying the Dragon and placed the gift in the center of his desk. The mail guy grinned and saluted as she left for her desk. When Mitch returned, his office would be full of brightly colored balloons with a gallant knight slaying a dragon center stage.

An hour later, Mitch exited the board meeting and gave her the thumbs up before heading toward his office. Waving back, she smiled to herself. She'd recused herself from the meeting to take care of Mitch's gift knowing full well the heart of the board.

A shout of exclamation from the other side of the floor caused her lips to curl in a grin. Chad, the mail guy, pushed his cart down the hallway pausing just long enough to wink. Isabella pushed away from her desk. Grabbing her coffee mug as an excuse to get a closer look, she headed down the hall toward the breakroom.

The sound of popping balloons, grunting and muttering sent joy through her spine. What would he think of the statue? Caitlyn stopped into the breakroom with her own coffee mug and jerked her head toward Mitch's office.

"What on earth do you think happened in there?" she mused. "Someone is taking the Secret Santa thing to the whole next level." She eyed Isabella for a moment. "So, is it true…?" She asked as she reached for the coffee pot and poured a cup.

Isabella froze. "Is what true?" The question held so many possibilities.

"Word around the office is that you and Mitch are dating." She leaned against the counter and took a long sip of her straight black coffee. "Any truth to the rumor? Whoever snags that man is a lucky girl, even with the bump in the road he hit recently. I certainly tried, but he ran for the hills."

Isabella felt the blood rush to her cheeks. She nodded. "Yes, since the night of the big game a couple weeks ago. We knew each other a long time ago from a college Bible study, but I never thought he looked my way. We've reconnected. Honestly, it's been remarkably amazing."

Caitlyn took another sip before setting her mug on the breakroom table. "Well, I wish you the best, girl. You deserve it. You're kind of the *unsung hero* of the office, you know." She reached over and grabbed Isabella's hand and cocked her head in thought. "or maybe you don't know." She squeezed then released her hand.

"Everyone around here knows they can count on you, Isabella. You always have a kind word even amidst deadlines and crunch times. Besides…" she thumbed toward Mitch's office. "Do you hear the man? Only you can get away with simultaneously frustrating him and pulling him out of his funk."

Isabella opened her mouth to interject, but Caitlyn stopped her. "Don't deny it. You're talking with an investigative journalist remember," she chuckled. "I know a secret about a Secret Santa, but your secret is safe with me," she winked, grabbed her mug and slipped out of the breakroom only to squeeze past Mitch entering with his unicorn mug and an adorable frown.

Isabella bit back her laughter and offered him a chair. He plopped down and stuck out his mug, a dazed look about his face. Isabella let a light laugh ring out as she took his empty mug and filled it.

"You look a bit stunned, Sir Robin… I've seen you in high society, as a crazed sports fan, climbing a rock wall, conquering a client and winning over the board; but this face… what rocked your world?"

Mitch turned brown, puppy dog eyes her direction. "My Secret Santa struck again. I fought a battle just to get to my desk only to get there and find the most amazing statue of a knight slaying a dragon. I'm pretty sure the cost is far beyond the Secret Santa parameters. I'm stunned."

"Did he leave a note?"

Mitch tossed the typed note across the table.

COURAGE…

YOU HAVE IT IN YOU.

WATCHING YOU SLAY DRAGONS IS A PLEASURE

~Your Secret Santa

"Is there a problem? I think the note describes you very well."

Mitch ducked his head and rubbed the back of his crown with his hands mussing his dark hair into a bedhead look. Adorable…

"Well, for starters, whoever the gifter is makes me look bad. I delivered a couple of gift-cards to my two Secret Santa recipients today. I'm not that creative. Whoever got *my* name is amazing! And then… I'm not sure I can live up to the whole knight in shining armor bit. What if I get knocked off the horse and disappoint? Instead of a knight, I feel like a grumpy old troll who just finally crawled out into daylight."

Isabella threw her head back as joyous laughter spilled out at the picture Mitch painted of himself. Nothing could be further from the truth, but he just didn't see it. He really didn't see the confident, warrior heart that he carried with him every day into every situation.

Rinsing out her coffee mug, she patted his

shoulder as she headed toward the door. "Hey, if I were a damsel in distress, I'd bank on you coming to my rescue every time. Gotta run… I have a lot of paperwork to do before the holidays to get our new client outlined for the next year. Keep slaying dragons, Mitch. One dragon at a time."

~

Mitch pulled into his assigned parking place for his apartment and stopped. Just stopped. Peace. The swirl of snowflakes caught up by the wind reminded him of his heart. So much change and no time to process… He needed a moment. Cold seeped into the parked car. He shivered.

Best take my moment inside, he reasoned. Grabbing his bag of burgers and fries, he lowered his head to the wind and made for the door. Inside, the cold beckoned him to change into his sweats and turn up the heat. He pulled a chair up to the window, took a bite of his burger and watched the snow fall.

The burger reminded him of Isabella or Marion… He wiped a small drop of ketchup from his chin and pondered her revelation. Did keeping her identity a secret bother him? Snagging a fry, he shrugged off the thought. He understood her quandary. Did her wealth and power hurt his ego?

Okay, be honest, Mitch ole' boy. After the fact, your pride took a bit of a beating. The offer of Editor-in-Chief went a long way in helping that department. He thought of the pain of the last year and the powerless feelings with which he struggled.

As Editor, he could do a lot of good. The thought settled.

Watching the snow continue to fall as darkness fell soothed his soul. For tonight, peace reigned, and hope settled. The merry lights of a Christmas tree in a window across the courtyard caught his eye and turned his thoughts toward his Secret Santa. Tomorrow, all would be revealed.

Though not the most creative, he managed to get Caitlyn a team jersey for the Royals, and Adeline tickets to a Broadway production he heard her long for in the breakroom. He thought they were pleased with their gifts. But *his* Secret Santa incited buzz in the entire office. If anyone knew the culprit, no one snitched. Everyone he surveyed seemed clueless.

From Isabella, he discovered that the game was completely blind. No master list existed. People simply drew names out of a hat… well, all but him. The last two names landed with him. Anyone could be his Secret Santa.

Gathering his trash, he turned out the lights and headed toward the bathroom to get ready for bed. Tomorrow, he would truly thank his Secret Santa for starting him back down the path of the hopeful. He planned to wear the tie to the Christmas party in honor of the changes brought about by the game.

Morning dawned bright and early. Mitch slapped the buzzing alarm and wiping a tired hand over his face, headed toward the automatic coffeemaker to pour a large cup. Last night, dreams of dancing presents and a line-up of Secret Santas threatened his career if he couldn't identify the true

Santa. He shook off the dream and yawned missing his crazy unicorn mug. He reached for his old college mug. He chuckled.

Who would have thought that unicorn tail would be such a great fit for my hand!

One look out the window proved the snow reached record amounts. He reached for his coffee and his Bible. Quiet time with His Lord always came first, in good seasons and bad ones. After reading, praying and finishing his coffee, he checked his watch. Good. Twenty minutes for a quick shave and change of clothes allowed him extra time to reach the office.

Five minutes later, the phone rang.

"Isabella?"

"Mitch, I'm so grateful I caught you," her voice sounded breathless over the phone. "On our side of town, heavy snowfall fell, but where the office is located, things are impassible. I've called off work for today. Having the office party isn't worth the risk to people's lives, plus the power and heat are out at the building. I told everyone to mail their Secret Santas a Christmas card and work from home. We'll celebrate after the first of the year. At least the Christmas edition and the Monday paper were put to bed last night. It buys us some time."

A sudden thought struck him. "Isabella... where are you?! Are you safe?"

A chuckle echoed through his phone. The reception flickered in and out. "About that..." Isabella's cheery voice spilled with laughter. "Would you believe I just got stuck right outside your apartment building? May I come up? I have that surprise I asked if I could give you."

A quick glance around the apartment, and Mitch winced. Oh, cleanliness graced every surface, but nary a Christmas decoration could be found. He looked like the grinch. Oh well, time to face the music. He couldn't let the love of his life stand dancing in the cold.

"Sure, let me buzz you in. Apartment 5, upstairs…"

"Actually, if you could help me, I'd appreciate it."

Grabbing his jacket, he headed down the stairs, stopping abruptly at the sight of a lovely snow princess standing at his gate. Her Jeep sported a tied-up Christmas tree, and her hands were full of decorations. His jaw dropped. How did she know?

The look on his face must have been obvious, for her good-natured laughter rolled over the last of his weary spirit. He began to laugh with her.

"Is this all for me?" he questioned cautiously.

She tilted her head and grinned. "Well… yes and no… I intended to add a surprise tree to the breakroom this morning when the weather turned me around. The roads got better this direction, so I made an educated guess on whom I could bless with Christmas. You came to mind, Sir Robin. Let me guess… not one ornament or tree? Am I right?"

He winced visibly. "You caught me. Guilty as charged." He grabbed the tree and threw it over his shoulder. She locked her car and followed him with the box of lights and decorations.

An hour later, lights, music and a well-decorated evergreen filled his home. He glanced over at the woman who changed his life adding one more ornament to the already full tree. She brought joy to everything she did. Grabbing her hand, they stepped back together to admire his new Christmas tree. Lights sparkled on the ceiling, and a beautiful glow filled the air. He hugged his benefactor tight with one arm as they soaked in the beauty.

"You know, I was looking forward to the reveal today. I'm blessed with an amazing Secret Santa. I wanted to let the person know how much God used the gifts, even my crazy unicorn mug, the bull-frog… everything, to restore hope in my life."

He sighed. "I guess we'll just have to wait until the roads clear." Isabella gave him a playfully, knowing look.

"I can tell you if you like. I know who your Secret Santa is…"

He raised an eyebrow and pulled her onto the sofa beside him. "Oh really… and how would you know that?"

She tossed him an innocent look meant to distract. "Could it be because I'm the assistant?"

He shook his head.

"Could it be because I'm the boss?"

Again, he slowly shook his head.

"Maybe its because *I'm* your Secret Santa, Mitch…"

He jerked back and studied her face.

"What?! I thought you weren't part of the game!"

She grinned. "Well, Howard backed out and… I knew you'd be the last one to turn in your form. I told you that I'd been tasked to give to one person.

All the other forms were passed out by the time you *finally* turned in your list."

He shook his head to clear the cobwebs. "But you didn't use any of my suggestions…"

She gave a merry laugh. "Hmm… let's see. White socks. WD-40, a gas can, and bottled water. Really, Mitch… You tried so hard to be difficult. Helping you see happily ever after in life again brought me such great joy, but I never dreamed you'd be my happily ever after too!"

He reached for her and pulled her close pressing his lips to hers. When he pulled away, she pressed her fingertips to her lips in joy. Suddenly, she kissed him again. He threw back his head in joy and praise to God.

"You are a gift, Lady Marion, my Queen Isabella," he whispered in her ear.

She pulled back and grinned. "About that… I have your final Secret Santa gift *with* me. Want to open it?" She snatched a package from behind the tree and held the package high. "But you have to read the card first…"

He grabbed the box like a kid at Christmas and began to shake the gift before looking at the tag. Something clunked and rattled. Isabella reached out a cheerful hand to stop him.

"Just read the card, Mitch."

Tilting his head, he turned over the gilded envelope to read.

> *Mitch,*
> *The keys to the kingdom are yours.*
> *Choose your legacy…*

With a quizzical glance, Mitch paused to study her.

"What's this?" he asked cautiously.

"Just open the box before I take the gift back!" Isabella insisted.

Nodding, Mitch hurriedly ripped the red and gold paper. Lifting the lid, he sobered and quickly sought Isabella's face. "Are these…?"

A slow smile curved at the corners of her rosy lips. "I'm sure you noticed the fairytale theme along the way…?"

He nodded with a grin of his own. "How could I miss it… a live frog in a bag of chocolate kisses…? A knight on a horse slaying a dragon… Definitely unforgettable," he teased.

Isabella tossed him a sassy look from beneath her long dark lashes and stuck one hand on her hip in adorable irritation. "Each gift served to bring you to this moment. In fact, I designed the entire office Secret Santa game in hopes of bringing you to *this* moment."

Mitch let the thought settle. She created the entire game for *him*?

"You put the entire office through the paces just to pull me from the doldrums? Am I really *that* pathetic?" he muttered and set the box on the table to meet her eyes. "I bet I'm the laughing stock of the whole office!" The office chuckles and laughter of the past few weeks suddenly seemed cynical as old panic threatened to rise. In a visceral reaction, he shoved the box from him causing the package to fall from the coffee table to the carpeted floor.

Isabella visibly paled, reached for the box and

set the lid back into place before standing. "Apparently, I overreached," her voice barely reached a whisper. "I've been told I do that on occasion. The board has definitely made that clear. My apologies. I wish you a very Merry Christmas. The late shift finished the Christmas edition just before the storm hit, so take a long holiday weekend. I'll see you at the office Tuesday…"

She grabbed her purse and paused in the doorway. "Tuesday, when everyone returns, there will be changes in the office. From now on, at the board's insistence, I will be Marionette Goldberg, Editor-in-Chief- media mogul." With resignation, she sighed. Her carefree spirit visibly tucked deeper away, placed like her lovely long hair into a confining, tight ball of exhausting self-control.

What have I done? Mitch panicked. "Isabella, wait!"

She shook her head in sorrow and paused with a sigh. "The snow stopped falling an hour ago. I have a lot of unexpected things to take care of. I truly need to go. Your response has thrown the contingency plan into play. I'm not prepared. I'll see you, Tuesday."

When she shut the door and stepped out into the cold, he froze unable to follow, unsure of how he allowed things to spiral in such a short time. When he snapped to his senses, he raced for the street. He stared dejected at an empty street.

Chapter Eight

All evening he called her cell phone, panicking with every hour that ticked by. How could he have even entertained the thought that she set him up for humiliation? Where did that idea even come from? Frustrated, he started a pot of coffee to keep his hands busy. The whole house mocked him. Every twinkling light, Christmas ornament and… a small gilded square on the coffee table caught his eye.

Stepping back into the living area, he reached for the envelope. Realization hit. He never even opened it! The outside of the envelope gave him the keys to the kingdom in fitting fairytale theme… until he opened the box and saw the keys to the entire media conglomerate and newspaper office and the truth of the casual, fairytale statement stepped out of the fairytale and into reality.

She officially gave him the *keys to her kingdom!* Yes, he'd been interviewed by the board, offered the Editor-in-Chief position, but the sight of the keys stopped him dead in his tracks. He recognized more than just the keys to the paper. That keyring held keys that unlocked the entire media empire:

radio, 24-hour cable news network, internet broadcasting, bill-boards and more. Momentarily overwhelmed, he spiraled into a panic.

He shook his head at his own stupidity and carefully tore open the gold envelope Isabella left behind. One glance at the inside and he melted into a puddle. Could he feel any lower? She gave him access to every ounce of her father's empire that she possessed, told him to now create his *own legacy* with it, and if he needed more, she offered the greatest thing of all…

He glanced down at the open envelope. Surprisingly, no card appeared, just a gold keychain with a ruby heart set inside a gold crown and an ancient key. A small gold label hung alongside the emblem. The inscription struck his heart. He dropped to the sofa and covered his head in his hands.

King of my heart… the inscription read. She offered her kingdom, her father's legacy and her heart. The greatest gift he would ever receive, and he'd dumped her offering on the floor like trash and accused her of intentionally humiliating him after all she'd down to restore him and set him in a place of power. As one of the most powerful women in the world, she offered to share the power with him, yet he walked away and let her carry the burden alone.

God, what do I do?

Forget your pride, your fears and step into the future I designed. Go to her.

Father, I've made a mess of things.

For all have sinned and fallen short of the

glory of God. Go.

He stood and grabbed his coffee, jacket and wallet and headed out the door. He would start with her condo. Then try the office. Urgency grew… he'd try the office first.

~

Snow began to fall again as Isabella pulled out onto the now deserted streets. The windshield wipers couldn't keep up with the swirling white mass. A scornful laugh escaped her lips at the irony. Her foolish heart couldn't keep up with her swirling emotions either. She squinted against the darkening sky and the fog of the glass. Slowing the car upon entering the overpass, she strained to shove the emotions aside and focus.

Suddenly, the steering wheel jerked out of her hand and the car careened across invisible black ice toward the guardrail. She shot up a prayer for Mitch and the office. Who would take care of the media empire when she died? Only God knew. Peace came as metal struck metal and the car teetered. Head met steering wheel. Light went dark.

Moments later, the flickering radio announced the highway and bridge closing until further notice.

An hour later, slumped over the steering wheel of her Jeep, Isabella stirred amidst bone-chilling cold. She blinked and tried to remember events leading up to her current predicament and drew a blank. Bad enough, a cut over her eye bled profusely, her left hand felt numb and her right foot ached and might be pinned under the crush of her crumbled car.

Moving to reach for her purse in the passenger seat, the car visibly wobbled. She froze and looked out through the cracked windshield to the sight of nothing but air… She let the tears flow; certain the day couldn't get any worse. Sending up a heart cry to her heavenly Father, she pondered her next move. Help wasn't coming; she couldn't move, yet she couldn't stay. A tiny spark of inspiration struck. Slipping her left arm next to the door, she managed to tug the seat lever and lower the back of her seat.

Unbuckling, she carefully scooted her body backwards on the seat back. She cried out. Her pinched foot hindered all progress. After five minutes of turning her ankle painfully, she managed to pull loose. She tried again and this time managed to inch her body back until she unzipped the plastic from the back window and slid all the way out into the blinding snow.

With no purse, no cell phone, no car, no help, no Mitch… what should she do? Her head ached as her memory of the past few hours rushed back. She'd offered Mitch everything, yet he seemed unable to accept. Loneliness threatened to overwhelm her. The heaviness of her father's legacy fell fully back on her shoulders. And Mitch… like the others before him, let pride and the weight of the burden overwhelm him causing all responsibility to fall back on her.

Isabella straightened her shoulders and tried to wipe the blood from her eyes. Her life mattered. Maybe she should finally sell the company, but honest, dedicated men were hard to find. She wouldn't turn the business over to just anyone. Shoving tomorrow's worries aside, she focused on the moment.

The temperature grew colder by the moment. She glanced up toward the heavens at the snowfall. With no sign of letting up, she needed a plan. Edging her way carefully around the back of the car to the passenger's side, she peered through the window at her purse. A shimmer of gold caught her eye on the seat next to the door. Could she reach her cellphone? The purse hung out of range.

Carefully, she unlatched the door and paused. The car shivered. Positioning her body at the best possible angle to reach the phone and jump back, she gently pulled the door open a crack and waited again. The phone sat just inches away. The car shook but remained unmoved. Reaching the few inches to the phone, she managed to pick it up. Her eyes fell on her purse, a foot away, the strap wrapped around the stick-shift. Temptation beckoned. The Spirit warned.

Choosing to be content with the phone, she pulled back and away from danger. Finally, things were looking up. Isabella turned on the phone, and hope died. Two percent… enough for one call, maybe two. She tried 911. Busy… She tried again. Busy… The phone showed one percent charge left. Call Mitch or call her driver?

Both choices left something to be desired. On Christmas Eve, the employee spent time with his large, boisterous family. The chances of his hearing the phone would be low. After their falling out, she really didn't want to call Mitch, yet… his gentlemanly side would force him to answer and come to her rescue.

Looking around, she moaned. The industrial side of town held few if any places to call for help. All businesses were closed, there were no gas stations and only one fast food restaurant several miles away.

Okay, Lord. I'll set my foolish pride aside and call Mitch.

She pulled up his number and dialed. No answer… his recorded voice came on compelling her to leave a message. She let him know her location and mentioned the fast food location as a second option. Her phone died. She slumped against the guardrail allowing herself one moment of pity-party. With no phone and Mitch out of reach, the time for action arrived.

She pulled her winter coat close, grateful for the gloves she'd stuffed in the pockets and set out.

~

The drive to the newspaper office slowed to a complete stop just before the overpass. Mitch pounded the steering wheel in frustration knocking his phone to the floorboard of the passenger's seat. He kicked himself for the hundredth time. If he lost her… the company, promotion, money meant nothing compared to his Isabella. Had he ruined his chances by his stupid overreaction?

His cell phone rang from the floor just as the car behind him honked. A policeman motioned him to get moving and make a U-turn. He did so, then pulled over at the nearest stop to snag his phone.

Though he'd called more times than he could count, he still hoped Isabella would call. His heart pounded at the notification. Isabella? She'd tried to call!

He dialed her number, but got no answer. Just knowing she'd called gave him peace. At least she remained safe in this mad house. He decided to head home and try her later. He'd make things right. They'd have Christmas together... his mind followed a pleasant direction as he drove back toward his apartment. Almost home, a thought occurred. Could Isabella have left a message?

He pulled forward when the light turned green and drove the last two blocks to his home before checking. Once the car came to a stop, he checked his screen for a message, please to find one. Climbing the stairs, he opened the recording. Halfway through, he sprang into action. According to her information and his attempt to cross the bridge, he knew he'd have to get creative if he were to reach her.

Inspiration struck as he scrambled in his apartment for a few essentials before heading out. A thermos containing the rest of his coffee, a couple blankets and an extra pair of socks and sweats, the first aid kit and matches just in case. A quick phone call to a buddy and he secured better transportation. Snatching up Bella's royal keychain and his Christmas present to her on his way out the door, he headed off into the night.

Moments later, he swapped transportation with his friend and made his way toward the bridge. The lone policeman nodded as he passed while still directing others to turn back. Mitch breathed a sigh of relief... until he saw Bella's Jeep. His heart nearly stopped at the sight of her red Jeep crushed and teetering over the bridge.

Thank you, God, for getting her out alive!

Obviously, lingering for help proved problematic. After playing phone tag, she must have set out on foot to the fast food location. Her footprints were fast disappearing in the storm. He followed her path as best he could for another twenty minutes until suddenly, a hunched over form appeared in the distance. Isabella...? The figure stumbled. Pulling over, he leaped to the rescue and gathered his damsel in distress into his arms.

The ride back might prove difficult, but he'd found her.

Isabella awakened to the odd sensation of swaying and bumping. Strong arms cradled her and offered shelter and warmth even as snowflakes continued to fall on her cheeks. She blinked and for the second time in a matter of hours, tried to make sense of her surroundings. The comfort of Mitch's five o'clock shadow filled her view. She snuggled closer afraid the dream would end. Where were they?

Realization came. The swaying, bumping... her wrecked car... Mitch's presence. She'd called. He came... on a horse! On a *white* horse, unless her eyes deceived her!

A low moan reached her ears.

"Mi Bella, I'm so sorry for over-reacting to your precious gift. You offered so much more than the

Editor-in-Chief position, set up the whole Secret Santa idea to bring me out of my shell and reminded me that God still brings 'happily-ever-afters'. I freaked out. I never intended to knock the gift over… never planned to reject it… but I let fear get the best of me. And when I found your greatest gift, the gift of your heart… I couldn't reach you.

I love you, Isabella. Can you forgive me? I want to bear your burdens and hold you close. Even if you never offer the keys to the kingdom again, I desire to hold the key to your heart."

The sincerity in his voice melted her heart. Oh, how she loved this man. Words refused to come, so she squeezed his hand. Her eyelids felt heavy. She needed to sleep.

Bright sunlight filtered through the window of her bedroom when Isabella finally blinked awake. Caitlyn sat reading in a chair at the foot of her bed and looked up.

"Aww… so the sleeping princess finally awakes. You worried us for a bit." She pointed to Isabella's head. Touching it made her wince.

"You cut your scalp in the wreck," Caitlyn explained. "And you definitely made the news… Marion Isabella Goldberg…" her friend waved off any coming explanation. "Mitch explained, so save your strength. All is well."

Isabella breathed a sigh of relief and forced herself to sit up. Everything hurt. "Who is… taking care of everything? I have to get to the office or at least contact the board so someone can fill in…"

Raising her hand, Caitlyn interjected. "It's being handled. You rest."

A knock on her bedroom door startled her, but Caitlyn seemed to expect it.

"My relief is here. Have a great day. I've got to get to work. The boss gets a little cranky about deadlines these days," she chuckled then sobered. "Seriously, Isabella. I'm glad you're okay. We all are," she added.

She left the room just as Mitch stepped in looking *fabulous* in a three-piece suit and his new exclusive silk tie. He looked every inch the imposing king of an empire. Concern blanketed his handsome face as he stepped to her bedside and reached for her hand.

"Isabella, darling! You're awake! Praise God. I almost lost you!"

She smiled. "Darling, huh?"

A sheepish grin formed at his lips. He shrugged and kissed her forehead. "I love you, darling. And I plan to keep telling you. The doctor said if you awakened that you could get up and move around as long as you take it easy for the rest of the day. I have a lot to tell you. I brought coffee… think you are able to join me in your living room?"

How could she resist? "Give me about fifteen minutes, please."

He nodded and stepped out of her room.

A few minutes later, with a stiff body and a bit of a headache, she stepped into her living room. The Christmas tree sparkled with multi-colored lights and carols sounded softly over the radio. The smell of coffee and cinnamon rolls filled the room. She breathed in the moment. Mitch stood by her small fireplace.

"May I get you coffee and a roll?" His voice held a touch of pleading that she couldn't resist. Plus, being waited on by someone who cared felt good. It had been a while.

"Yes, please," her voice softened.

Taking the coffee cup and small plate he brought over, she looked up at her rescuer. "I love you, Mitch," she whispered. "Did you really show up to my rescue on a white horse, or did I dream you carried me on horseback?

His eyes twinkled. "A very reliable mode of transportation in a snowstorm when coming to the rescue." Worried brown eyes shot to hers. "I botched things royally and almost lost you because of it. I love you, Marion Isabella. I can't imagine life without you."

Rising carefully, she came to him. Tears glistened in his eyes. Her own vision blurred with tears as well. "Life is not without it's bumps, Mitch. Would you really want me? I come with a complicated package. It's too much for most people. In fact, I've considered selling… I just can't find an honest, hard-working person to take over. I…"

He stopped her with a finger to the lips. "I'm here now, Bella. If you'll have me… we're in this together, or… I will carry your load completely if you want out. If you want to sell, I still just want you, darling."

He dropped to one knee in front of the lovely Christmas tree. Her heart pounded. In light of everything, did her heart desire him?

"Yes!"

He raised a handsome eyebrow. "I haven't asked you anything yet?" he teased.

"Then yes to whatever you ask, Mitch." He laughed. "That is quite the blank check you just handed over, Mi Bella. How about a lifetime of love, adventure and faith, together through whatever God sends our way? Would you do the honor of becoming my wife?"

"YES!"

He stood and held her close. She could feel his care with her bruises, but she wanted more. Standing on tiptoe, she tugged his lips to hers. He grinned and complied. A moment later, he pulled back with twinkling eyes and held up a small velvet box. "Though I love your priorities, darling, do you think you'd like the ring?"

With a squeal, she kissed his lips again before opening the box, a princess cut diamond graced the center of a gold setting.

"Mi Bella… in Christ, we will create our happily-ever-after. Real life can be better than a fairytale when we follow His plan and love each other whole-heartedly. Be mine?"

"Always."

He kissed her nose. "Now, rest, my love. I've a paper to put to bed, but I'll be back to check on you. Any requests?"

"A Christmas wedding?"

He looked disappointed. "You want to wait a whole year? Well, anything for you…"

She chuckled and interrupted. "This Christmas."

His startled eyes shot to hers. "Today…?!" he croaked.

"Think we can secure a license, preacher and a few single friends? I have connections!" she teased.

"I thought I am the impractical one! How about I be the tiny voice of reason...? New Year's Eve? It'll give you time to recover, and I'll make all the arrangements. Deal?"

"Perfect, Mitch. I can't wait to share a lifetime with you. Burdens, challenges, and happily-ever-afters. In Christ, together, we can thrive in this crazy world."

"You know it!" He kissed her gently. "He alone brings the hope to every story. I look forward to see what He brings in the next chapter."

Stephanie Guerrero has written ten novels or novellas, is a member of ACFW, a middle school teacher, pastor's wife, children's minister, & mother of four amazing kids ages 13 to 21. She adores the Lord, her husband, dark chocolate, travel, the great outdoors, and happily-ever-after.

'Choose joy in the midst of crazy' is her latest motto.

She loves to hear from readers.

You can find her on Facebook at:

Stephanie Guerrero, author,

or email her at

whitedragonblackjade@gmail.com

Made in the USA
Columbia, SC
21 November 2019